P9-ELR-775

Summerdog
Comes
Home

GEORGE A. ZABRISKIE writes and produces films together with his wife, Sherry. Many of their films are for children, including *THE SECRET SQUINT*, *WHAT IS A TREE?*, *BOSWELLES*, *BON VOYAGE*, *FAR AWAY AND LONG AGO*, and their first feature film, *SUMMERDOG*. Mr. Zabriskie has written articles for *The New York Times*, *Moneysworth*, and *New Hampshire Profiles*. SUMMERDOG COMES HOME *is his first novel.*

George A. Zabriskie

SUMMERDOG COMES HOME is an original publication of Avon Books.
This work has never before appeared in book form.

AVON BOOKS
A division of
The Hearst Corporation
959 Eighth Avenue
New York, New York 10019

Published by arrangement with the author.
Library of Congress Catalog Card Number: 79-55577
ISBN: 0-380-75259-x

Photography by George and Sherry Zabriskie

First Camelot Printing, April, 1980

Printed in the U.S.A.

To Zoe the real “Hobo” and
to Sherry, Oliver, and Tavia
who worked so hard and
never lost the faith

CONTENTS

INTRODUCTION

The book and the motion picture *Summerdog* follow the adventures of the Norman family and their adopted dog, Hobo. But Hobo was a middle-aged mutt when Adam Norman rescued him from the raccoon trap. What had happened to Hobo before he came to live with the Normans? Where did he come from? Whom had he lived with?

Summerdog Comes Home tells the story of Hobo's life before he met the Normans. He lived with a number of families who all called him different names. So this is the story of "Fluffy," "Bounce," "Sam," and "Shag," who are, of course, all Hobo, the Summerdog.

PART ONE
ABANDONED

THE DAY STARTED LIKE EVERY DAY HAD FOR the past month. As soon as Jill was awake, Hobo jumped up on her bed. Since Jill was ten years old, there was lots of room. Hobo found his favorite place at the foot of the bed. He turned around and around until he had scrunched up the blankets into a comfortable nest. Then, curling himself up with his nose on his hind paw, he gave a great sigh and pretended to be asleep.

Jill sat up and said, "Silly old Shag, you're a dog, not a bird, you know." She had named him Shag because he was so shaggy. Jill hugged him and told him how much she loved him. Then he nuzzled his cold nose into her neck, which they both enjoyed very much.

Everything was going along, just like always on this particular morning, except that Jill held Hobo for an extra long time, and when she finally did let go and climb out of bed, she was crying. "You go and take your morning run and I'll fix your breakfast." She tried to say it very positively, but she was sniffling back tears at the end.

Jill opened the squeaky screen door and Hobo trotted out into the already hot summer day. He heard the screen door slam behind him. Only then did he turn and watch Jill disappear into the kitchen. Hobo always felt uncomfortable when people cried, particularly when it was a person he cared about. He didn't understand tears. He didn't know what to do to make the person feel better. The day was so full of good smells and bright sunshine and here was Jill crying, for no reason at all that he could figure out. Well, one thing he did know, tears didn't last very long. Whatever the problem was, it always seemed to solve itself.

He trotted around to the back of the house. The cottage was surrounded by woods. The only break in the trees was where the narrow dirt road wound its way up from the blacktop to the cottage clearing. Hobo's nose told him that raccoons had been around again last night and that a number of deer had crossed by the edge of the clearing. Having spent all his life in the city, Hobo found these country animal smells new and exciting.

On the other side of the cottage, Hobo saw Jill's parents putting a lot of their things into the car. The things still had some of their city scent to them, except for a big plastic bag of garbage. They were even taking the garbage!

Jill's mother saw Hobo and said, "Don't you think we should make some effort to . . ."

The man interrupted, "There isn't time. It's a long drive. He'll be all right. There's lots of food and somebody will take him in. Jill!" he shouted. "Hurry up! Your mother has your breakfast on the table. We've got to get going."

Something was wrong. Hobo felt it all around him now. This wasn't going to be like all the other days that he had spent with Jill and her parents at this cottage in the woods.

Jill called to him from the screen door. She had his bowl of breakfast for him on the porch, with his water bowl right beside it, just like always. He looked up at her. She was looking down at him. Then the tears came again and she got down on her knees and hugged him. "Shag, oh Shag, it's so unfair!"

Jill's mother came in now and told her nicely but firmly that this kind of behavior didn't help and that she must eat her breakfast and then they must be on their way. "You've had a wonderful time with Shag but, like all good things, it must come to an end. Now you knew that when we took him, so please, Jill, let's have no more tears."

Jill ate her breakfast and Hobo ate his and neither of them enjoyed their food very much. After breakfast Jill gave Hobo one last hug. Then she got into the car and drove away. Hobo was used to being left behind. The public beach at the lake nearby didn't allow dogs, so every time Jill and her parents went there, he was left at the cottage. He tried very hard to believe that this was what was happening now, but he couldn't. They never packed the car like that just to go to the lake. And Jill was always happy to go before. No, that couldn't be it. Hobo decided that he would just have to wait for them to come back.

The bright sunny day with its exciting smells had suddenly become unbearably hot and unpleasant. It was cooler in the cottage. Hobo trotted over to the screen door, caught the edge of it with his paw, and pulled. It had always opened before, but now it was locked. He tried again. It wouldn't open. He trotted around to the back door. It was locked too. Then he caught the scent of breakfast again. He followed the smell to the edge of the woods. There, in the shade of the trees, was his bowl piled high with food. His full water bowl was there too. This was very strange. He'd already had his breakfast. He sniffed at the food. It certainly smelled good. Normally he would have plunged in and treated himself to a second helping, but he just didn't feel like it today. He lapped up some of the water and flopped down in the shade of the trees to wait.

He must have dozed off because the next thing he knew, the sun was shining in under the trees and making him uncomfortably hot. Hobo got up and stretched. The sun had warmed up his food too. The good scent of the warm food was so strong that he was tempted to gobble it up. But again, he didn't have the heart for it. He trotted over to the shady side of the cottage and lay down in the dirt. He wasn't sleepy anymore. His nose worked over all the scents in the air. The house was empty, that was for sure. There was no car, no people, nothing but the sweet smell of the honeysuckle flowers that grew over one side of the porch. Then he heard the distant sound of a car on the blacktop. Maybe that was Jill and her parents coming back! The engine sound grew louder, reached a peak as the car passed the dirt road, and then faded away again down the blacktop.

Hobo got up and circled the house. He explored the edge of the woodline. He wandered down the dirt road to the blacktop. A truck rumbled by. He hung back in the brush by the side of the road. Trucks frightened him. They were too big and they made too much noise. It was getting dark anyway, so he returned to the cottage. He sniffed at his food, but he still wasn't hungry. He scratched out a place for himself in the dirt along the cool side of the house. He turned around and around to make himself a nest. It wasn't anywhere near as comfortable as the foot of Jill's bed. Nevertheless he curled up with his nose on his hind paw and went to sleep.

He slept fitfully. He thought he heard sounds of the car and Jill's voice. He wasn't sure whether he was awake or asleep. He kept thinking about, or maybe it was dreaming about, the good times he and Jill had had together: playing catch with sticks in the yard, chasing frogs into a small pond that was nearby, discovering their nearest neighbor in a similar cottage quite some distance away through the woods. Actually, that wasn't really so pleasant. The neighbor had a large, nasty bulldog/doberman mixed-breed mutt named Bruno. The beast had tried to run Jill and Hobo off the place until a woman called him inside. The woman was nice, though, and gave Jill some cookies and lemonade, while Hobo took a long, refreshing drink from Bruno's water bowl. As he slurped it up he could hear Bruno growling just inside the house. It felt strangely good to be helping himself to Bruno's water. It paid the beast back for being so unfriendly. That had been quite an adventure. Hobo drifted off to sleep remembering how good it was to be with Jill, curled up on her bed, being hugged and talked to. Those were the best times.

Angry chattering sounds and mean spitting noises shattered these dozey rememberings. Hobo jumped up. Raccoons were eating his breakfast! Worse than that, a skunk was challenging them! As always the skunk had his way. Now it was eating his breakfast! Hobo dashed over, growling as fiercely as he could. The skunk simply turned his back on Hobo, raised his tail, and that terrible stench hit the poor dog right in the face. His eyes stung. He cried in agony. He sneezed again and again but couldn't clear the stench from his nose. He tried panting through his mouth, but that was worse. His mouth began to foam. He couldn't swallow. He couldn't breathe. He felt like he was going to throw up. He did and then he felt a little better.

Hobo crawled away, back to his nest by the side of the cottage. He was one miserable dog. And it made him feel even worse to hear that skunk lapping up his breakfast and he not able to do a thing about it. Hobo barely endured the rest of the night. With the first rays of the early morning sun, Hobo got up and checked out his breakfast bowl. The skunk hadn't eaten all the food, but what was left stank so of skunk that the thought of eating it made Hobo feel sick all over again.

Hobo stayed at the cottage for three days, waiting for Jill and her parents to return. On the second day he even ate the skunk-smelling food, but there wasn't much of that. The second night it rained. Hobo thought the effect of the skunk attack had pretty much worn off, until his fur got wet; then he reeked of skunk all over again. But the rain also made puddles and he eagerly lapped up all the water he could get. By the end of the third day he was so hungry that all he could think of was food. He knew he couldn't stay at the cottage any longer.

Early the next morning he decided to go to the only place he knew where there would be people. Hobo knew that wherever there are people, there is garbage. And right now garbage sounded like a mighty fine breakfast. He started to make his way over to the neighbor's cottage. He tried not to think about Bruno. Maybe the beast would be inside or off in the car with the woman somewhere.

No such luck. As Hobo approached the edge of the woodline he could see Bruno patrolling the yard in a hostile manner. Hobo stopped to study the situation. There was a low shed attached to the back of the cottage. Hobo's nose told him that from this shed came the delightful aroma of leftover spaghetti with meat sauce, stale bread, and some cheese that had gotten a little too ripe for most humans, but best of all there was a steak bone! Hobo worked his nose very carefully over the warm summer air. Yes. For sure there was a steak bone with morsels of meat on it. And it was just about two days old. Perfect! That shed had to be the garbage shed, and he had to get in there.

But while Hobo was savoring these delicious smells, Bruno suddenly caught the scent of a strange dog with a touch of skunk about him. With a throaty growl the beast leaped at Hobo.

Bruno was bigger and faster, but Hobo was hungrier. Hunger lent wings to his feet and, being smaller, he could duck and turn quicker. In the woods he could dodge around the trees and bushes and stay ahead of Bruno's drooling jaws. But in the clearing around the cottage, Hobo knew he would be no match for Bruno. And he had to cross that clearing to get to the shed. While his hunger gave

Hobo spirit, it also made him tire sooner. He knew in the long run Bruno could catch him. Whatever he was going to do to get that steak bone, he had better do it soon.

Then, as he scooted out from behind a barberry bush, Hobo saw the garbage shed right in front of him, about fifty feet away. With one final burst of energy he made the dash across the open yard to the shed. Hobo was born a terrific jumper and having Bruno on his tail certainly helped. In one leap he made it to the top of the shed. In another he was on the roof of the cottage.

Bruno scrambled to the top of the garbage shed, but then, being a lot heavier, he lost momentum and slid back off the sharply sloping roof to the ground. The beast was furious. His angry barking and constant jumping up against the side of the cottage soon brought the woman out into the yard. Hobo flattened himself as close as he could to the hot tar paper roof. The woman looked up, but she didn't see him.

"Bruno! You bad boy! Have you chased a squirrel up on the roof again?"

Bruno's answer was another volley of furious barking and jumping up against the side of the cottage.

"Bruno! You stop that! You naughty dog! You're scratching the paint! You come inside right now."

The woman took Bruno by his choke chain collar and pulled. At first he resisted. He tried to back away. But the choke collar hurt, so he skulked along with her, making grumbling growling sounds and directing angry looks up toward the roof. The woman kept scolding him.

"You should be ashamed of yourself. A big, strong dog

like you chasing helpless little wild animals. I don't know what I'm going to do with you."

Hobo heard the screen door slam. He waited a few moments. Then, very quietly, he made his way to the edge of the roof, jumped down lightly onto the garbage shed and then down to the ground. He caught the edge of the door with his paw and pulled. The door swung open. In an instant he had overturned a plastic garbage can and gotten the morsel-laden steak bone in his teeth. He was feeling quite proud of himself as he trotted away toward the woods. Then he heard the squeak of the screen door again as it opened.

"Now, Bruno, if you will be a good boy and not chase any more squirrels, Mama will let you out to play in the yard again."

Hobo turned just in time to see the woman give that beast a loving pat and let him loose. What's worse, the beast saw Hobo. With a throaty growl and foaming mouth, Bruno leaped from the woman's hands. She screamed. Hobo dashed for the woods. Barking furiously, Bruno began to close the distance between them. That terrible sound was getting closer and closer. It was right behind him! Hobo saw a large barberry thicket looming up in front. Getting a firm grip on the steak bone, he dove into the thicket. It was a bramble of thorny branches, but Hobo's long hair protected his skin from the sharp barbs. He wriggled into the very center of the thicket and waited.

At first Bruno plunged in after Hobo, but the dog had very short hair. The thorny brambles scratched his skin. He jumped back and yelped in pain. He circled the thicket, barking and growling. But he could not get in. Hobo was safe, for the moment.

The woman continued calling from the cottage yard. At first Bruno paid no attention to her, but after a while, when she said that she would give him a doggie bone if he came back, he decided a bone in the hand was worth more than one in the bush, so he gave a few more nasty barks and then skulked back to the cottage. Hobo held the steak bone with his paws and licked it. It was delicious. Slowly he started to eat, savoring every morsel. To him, at this moment, it seemed to be the very best meal he had ever had.

Hobo stayed in the barberry thicket for a long time. He kept working over the steak bone, getting every bit of goodness out of it. Also, he was afraid to leave. He didn't know what to do or which way to go. His meal had made him thirsty. He wriggled out of the thicket. He knew that there was water somewhere near, deeper into the woods, away from the cottage. He decided that this was the best way to go.

Soon he came to a small brook. After quenching his thirst, he decided to cool himself off. He plunged into the sparkling stream and lay down, letting the water flow through his long shaggy coat. It felt so good that he hated to get out, but he didn't want to stay this close to Bruno's house for very long. He climbed out and gave himself a complete shakedown. Hobo's shakes always started with his whiskers, worked their way over the loose skin of his back, and ended with his tail. At any one moment, different parts of him would be shaking in different directions. It may have looked strange, but it shot a lot of water off very quickly. It also made him feel great. After a good meal, a cool bath, and a refreshing shake, Hobo was not afraid anymore. He was certain that he could handle whatever might come his way.

Since water was necessary for life, Hobo decided to stay near the brook. He put his nose up and his tail high. There was bounce in his step as he trotted off, following the brook upstream. Hobo had shaken, but he was still quite wet. Hobo wet and Hobo dry looked like two different animals. When his long hair was dry and fluffy, Hobo seemed to be about twice as big as he really was. His ears were topped with tufts of hair and his tail was one great plume. When he was wet he looked more like a slightly oversized water rat, with pointy little ears and a long skinny tail. But Hobo couldn't see himself trotting off, looking small and silly, while acting like he was king of the forest. And even if he could, he probably wouldn't have cared.

As he followed the stream, it began to get smaller and to run faster. The ground became steeper. Hobo was climbing a mountain. There were waterfalls in the stream now that splashed into little rocky pools. The ground was more rocky, too. The trees were fewer, but much bigger. Toward evening Hobo was surprised to discover that the stream suddenly disappeared between two rocks! He tried to hunt around behind the rocks to see where it went, but he couldn't find it anyplace. He returned to the spot where the water gushed out from between the rocks. It reminded him of the way water came out of the faucet in people's houses, only here there was much more water. He hoped nobody would turn it off! He took a few nervous laps of the icy cold, refreshing water just in case.

Hobo decided to spend the night by the spring and to

worry about which way to go in the morning. He made himself a comfortable nest in some pine needles and, with the murmer of the spring talking to him, he slept soundly for the first time since Jill went away.

He woke up the next day stiff and cold. He had never walked so much in one day in his whole life. He got up, rear end first, and stretched his front paws out in front of him as far as they would go. Every muscle ached. No one had turned off the spring, so he refreshed himself with a long, cool drink. Now it was breakfast time and, of course, there was no breakfast. Hobo worked his nose over the crisp, cool air. Not an enticing edible smell anywhere.

Then he heard a rustling in the pine needles not far away. A squirrel was searching for pine cones and eating the seeds out of them. Hobo watched, fascinated. Some memory from long, long ago came into his mind. Some instinct from his wild dog ancestors told him that the squirrel might just possibly be breakfast. He'd chased squirrels and pigeons before, and even frogs, with Jill, but he'd never actually caught one. All of that was just for fun. This was something else. This was serious breakfast business. Hobo froze. He didn't move a muscle, except for the tip of his nose. It twitched back and forth, trying to sort out the various scents in the air. Hobo watched and waited. The squirrel certainly didn't look like any breakfast that he had ever eaten. Breakfast, for him, had always come out of a can or a plastic bag. The squirrel didn't smell like breakfast either. It smelled just like a squirrel.

Now, without even knowing what he was doing, Hobo found himself stealthily creeping closer to that squirrel. Every muscle, every nerve in his body was concentrated on catching it. He moved ever so slowly. He crept closer and closer. Then Hobo pounced! Hobo almost caught him. There were even a few squirrel tail hairs under his paw. But the rest of the squirrel was up in the branch of a tall pine tree, chattering and scolding in a most annoying way. Hobo gave up and left.

He decided to keep going up the mountain. Going back down would only take him to Bruno's house and he didn't particularly want to tangle with that beast again. Maybe he could get better at stalking and pouncing. Maybe he was meant to be a hunter like his wild dog ancestors. Hobo rather liked this idea. But six uncaught squirrels later, Hobo had serious doubts about hunting down a breakfast in the wild. All he could think of was that bowl of food that Jill fixed for him every morning at the cottage. That was the good life. What had gone wrong? Why hadn't Jill and her parents come back? Hobo didn't have any answers, but he couldn't stop wondering about it.

Suddenly, he was aware that the walking was easier. The land was sloping down in front of him. He had crossed over the mountain. Then, just as suddenly, came the pungent scent of meat. It wasn't like the prepared meat that he was used to eating, but it wasn't like the squirrel either. This was more like the meat that people bring home from the store. He'd tasted it a few times when someone had tossed him trimmings from a steak or roast. This was the scent of uncooked fresh meat. As he got closer, another familiar scent came to him. He had sniffed it often in the early morning at the cottage. It was the scent of deer.

Then he saw it. A deer with a bullet hole through its chest. He could smell the gunpowder. It was a smell he didn't like and wouldn't forget. There were human scents too. Hunters had taken some of the meat and left the rest. The meat smelled delicious. Hobo started to help himself to some venison steak, when he was chilled to the bone by the most frightening sound that he had ever heard. It was a loud, snarling scream and it came from a tree right over his head. Hobo jumped back and looked up. There, on the lowest limb of the tree, was a huge bobcat shrieking at him.

Hobo backed off a little more, so he wouldn't be right under the big cat in case it decided to leap on him. He gave his most serious bark. It wasn't an angry, growling bark, like Bruno's. He didn't want to start a fight with the cat. But it wasn't his happy, yapping bark either. He didn't want the cat to take him for a fool. It was a bark that tried to say, "Look, there's enough here for both of us. I'll just have my breakfast and leave. Let's be reasonable and not make a big deal over this."

The bobcat, however, didn't get the message. He snarled again, showing off a big mouth full of teeth. Then he flexed his muscles, as if he were about to leap. Hobo curled his lips back and showed his teeth too as he gave a low, throaty, "Don't mess with me!" kind of growl. Hobo tried to make the growl as fierce as possible to show that he wasn't afraid of any cat. After all, he'd chased a lot of cats in his life. They had always run up onto something high, a fire escape or a tree to get away. They were always afraid of him. Why should he be afraid of this one? It didn't even have a tail. He growled again to reassure himself that he had the upper hand in this particular dog/cat situation.

The bobcat just looked down at him, showed his claws, and then, with one sweep of those claws, he ripped off a large piece of bark from the tree. Hobo was pretty impressed. What was it about this cat that made him so different from the others that he had chased? Well, for starters, it was bigger . . . a lot bigger. It was five or six times bigger than any cat Hobo had ever chased before. It was even bigger than Hobo. Its teeth were bigger too. And those claws were the sharpest claws Hobo had ever seen. Furthermore, it was already up a tree. Hobo could hardly chase it. But it could very easily chase Hobo. The thought of that cat coming after him with those teeth and those claws . . . it would be worse than Bruno. And, after all, this was the bobcat's territory. Hobo had no claim on that deer. He was just passing through. The more he thought about it, the less hungry he became and the more eager he was to be on his way. He directed one last serious bark up at the cat and showed his teeth, but only a little, more like a smile than a snarl. Then, keeping his eyes on the cat, he slowly backed away.

Sensing victory and wishing to make it certain, the bobcat let out a snarl and leaped out of the tree at Hobo. Hobo, however, was not there. That snarl had sent him on his way with one giant bound. His paws hardly touched the ground as he fled downhill, away from that fiercesome cat with no tail. The bobcat followed for a while to make sure this intruder would not return. But even after the bobcat quit the chase Hobo kept on running.

Hobo didn't stop until he had run all the way down the side of that mountain. The pads on his paws were sore from all the rocky ground that he had covered so quickly. He was out of breath and panting hard. He was tired, hungry, and very thirsty. It was midday now and hot. What was worse, a wide, new four-lane turnpike blocked his way. He was afraid to cross that wide stretch of concrete. The cars and trucks came by at such high speeds that the wind from them whipped his hair and the sound they made hurt his ears. He flopped down on his stomach, hind legs out back, forepaws in front, and tried to figure out what to do. He was certain that he was not going to try and cross that highway. Maybe if he followed alongside of it for a while it would end, or get smaller, or come to a town where there would be people. People had always been a part of his life, for better or worse, but he never realized how totally dependent he was on them, or their garbage, for his survival. He watched the traffic going past in both directions and wondered which way would be the best direction to go. Since he couldn't come up with any answer, he decided to go along with the traffic on his side of the highway. He hadn't gone very far before he turned back and went in the other direction. He hated the way the cars and especially the trucks roared up behind him. Every time they passed, he was sure they were going to run him down. He'd much rather face them head-on. That way he could be certain that they were not going to hit him. So he started off again facing the traffic.

He walked at a slow steady pace. He was still tired from his run down the mountain and he was very thirsty. When he came to some shade he rested. He caught the scent of water. It was a pond with frogs and turtles. He sniffed more carefully. It seemed to be right on the other side of the turnpike. He climbed back up the mountain a little way to make sure with his eyes. There it was, a small pond shimmering in the bright sunlight. He was so thirsty. He dashed onto the highway without looking or thinking; all he wanted was to get to that water. Suddenly, he heard the roar of a diesel engine, the blast of a horn, and the squeal of brakes. Hobo froze in fear. A huge trailer truck was right on top of him. Suddenly, the sun went out. He was surrounded by the dark blur of wheels turning. A huge, dark shape passed over him. The sound was deafening. The blast of wind turned him around and rolled him over. The stench of burning rubber from the brakes filled his nose and lungs. Then, just as suddenly, the roar and the smell and the blur of wheels was gone, moving away down the highway. The sun came back. He saw green grass and scrambled over to it and rolled down a gentle slope. He was in the center island between the two double lanes of the turnpike.

Hobo lay there in the grass for a long time. He couldn't quite believe that a huge trailer truck had run right over him. It hadn't touched him. He was still alive! Sometimes it pays to be small. He got up finally and shook himself. Everything seemed to be working, including his nose. He had been flipped around so much by the truck that he was no longer certain which side of the highway he had just crossed and which side he still had to cross. He stood there in the grass between two strips of concrete that looked exactly alike. Cars and trucks were rushing by him on either side. He was a very confused dog. It was his nose that straightened him out. After a few sniffs, he knew exactly where the pond was and which side of the turnpike he still had to cross.

This time he approached the concrete very carefully. He waited until there were no cars or trucks to be seen or heard. Then he dashed across the road and plunged into the pond on the other side. He swam out to the middle, lapping up the water as he went, very happy to be alive. His long, shaggy coat spread out all around him, supporting him in the water. He looked something like a giant, gray lily pad. He hardly had to paddle with his paws at all. It was cool and restful floating on the surface of the pond this way. After a few minutes, he was aware that there was a slight current in the pond. It was taking him over toward one end. He didn't care; in fact, it was pleasant to be gently carried along this way. Then his hind paws touched bottom. He was at the place where the pond overflowed and became a small stream. Now he knew what he must do. He must follow that stream until he came to some place where there were people. He might get very hungry on the way, but with the stream alongside he would not be thirsty again. He climbed out of the water, gave himself a good shake, and started to follow the brook downstream.

There were lots of frogs around. Whenever he saw one, he tried to catch it. The problem was that the frogs always saw him first. He never really saw them at all. He heard them as they splashed into the water. There were only a few times when he saw a frog sitting by the side of the brook before the frog saw him. Then Hobo would concentrate all his nerves and muscles on catching that frog. Hunkered way down, making himself as small as possible, moving ever so slowly, he would sneak forward. When he got close enough, he would pounce. But, every time, the frog would jump sooner and Hobo would hear that annoying splash in the water. All that afternoon, he never caught a single frog.

He slept that night in a nest that he made for himself in

the tall grass by the side of the brook. Even though the water made soft murmuring sounds, he did not sleep well. His dreams were full of huge, black, blurry wheels turning all around him, surrounding him, coming toward him, and full of sounds, loud roaring engine noises, blasting horns and screeching brakes which became the screaming snarl of the bobcat. Then the wheel, just before it ran over him, became the snarling cat's mouth full of teeth. He would wake up, with his legs twitching and his whole body shaking with fright. He had that same dream all night long.

With the first light of dawn, he continued on his way. He wanted to get as far away as possible from these terrible experiences and their frightening memories. He wandered alongside the brook all that day. He couldn't catch anything to eat. He was never thirsty, just terribly hungry. The water in the brook was the only thing that kept him going, that and the belief that if he could just keep walking long enough, he would find another home and another family where he would be loved and cared for. He tried to keep thinking about that. He slept soundly the next night. He was so tired that nothing could keep him from sleeping.

When he awoke, it was midmorning. He was so weak he could hardly get up. He noticed that he hadn't even bothered to make a nest for himself the night before. He staggered over to the brook and lapped up some water. He felt a little better, but the emptiness in his stomach was overwhelming. He tried eating some grass and leaves. He chewed the bark off some sticks and drank more water. Anything to stop his hunger. All it did was make him sick and then he felt worse. But he knew he must keep going. He must find a place where people were. He was not a wild animal. He knew that now, for certain. He had to be with people to survive.

He moved his paws forward mechanically, one after the other. He didn't care about the frogs jumping in the brook ahead of him. He didn't try to catch them anymore. It took everything he had just to keep moving, slowly forward, one paw after the other. He was no longer aware of the trees and bushes around him. He didn't care that he was entering a more wooded area. His nose told him that raccoons had been around. He didn't care about that either. He didn't care about anything except keeping going and staying near the brook. Without thinking, his paws moved forward, one after the other. Suddenly, he heard a snap and felt a terrible pain in his right front paw. Something hard and sharp had caught him. He wrenched to get free, but the metal trap only bit harder into his flesh. Hobo pulled away with all his might, but the trap was chained to a tree. He tried to bite the chain with his teeth. He tried to pull it off the tree. He tried to break it in two. But the more he tried to get loose, the more it hurt both his paw and his teeth. He thrashed around in agony on the muddy bank of the brook. Then his efforts grew weaker. Finally, he stopped trying to get free. He stopped trying to do anything. The pain in his paw was all that he knew. To stop that pain, his brain shut down and Hobo lost consciousness.

PART TWO
MEMORIES

FIRST NAME, "FLUFFY"

WHILE UNCONSCIOUS, LOTS OF GOOD FEELings came flooding to Hobo. Soft, furry bodies were all around him, cuddling against him, making happy little noises. There was one larger body that was more important than all the rest. It gave him warm, sweet milk. He could fill his tummy whenever he wanted. He was never hungry and never tired. He could curl up against that big, soft, furry body and take a nap anytime. Everything was good and warm and loving when Hobo was a puppy and had a mother who gave him everything he needed.

There were other puppies, too, his brothers and sisters in the litter. At first they, and their mother, were all in one box together. Hobo remembered the fun they all had pouncing on each other, climbing over their mother, playing King of the Mountain on her back, nuzzling into her long thick fur, and drinking that warm, sweet milk. Life in that box was just about perfect.

At first the mother was the only one who could get out of the box. It was like she just disappeared. Hobo wondered what happened to her. It made him uneasy when she left. But she always came back. He wondered what it was like outside the box. One day, Hobo discovered that he could climb up on one of his brother's backs and scramble over the edge of the box. He was the first puppy to get out.

It was a very different place outside the box. It was big and empty, with many strange smells and peculiar shapes. There were four chairs around a table, all painted white. There was a big, white box that made a whirring sound and a smaller white box with a door in the front and something on top that was making a gurgling sound. The place smelled of detergent and food. Hobo was timidly taking all this in, when his mother appeared from the next room, picked him up gently in her mouth, and carried him back to the box. His mother dropped him in among his brothers and sisters and then climbed in the box herself. That ride, being held up high by the scruff of his neck, was the most exciting thing that had happened to him in his whole life so far. He decided to get out of the box as often as he could.

He was big enough to just be able to look over the side of the box. None of his brothers or sisters had been outside, so they weren't so interested in what went on out there. But Hobo was very interested. He watched a woman come into the room and open the big box that made the whirring sound. Inside were shelves filled with many things of different shapes and colors. The woman took a small box, unwrapped a paper covering, and dumped what was inside into the gurgling pot. The gurgling stopped. Then the woman left the room.

Hobo was fascinated. He had to know what was going on. His mother was asleep along one side of the box. Hobo climbed up on her back, stretched his front paws to the top edge of the box, and jumped. He landed hard on the kitchen floor. Cautiously, he sneaked over toward the pot that had started gurgling again. Little white puffs of cloud came up and disappeared. Something smelled good. He got as far as the table when the woman returned. He stayed under the table and watched. The woman took a lid off the pot, stuck in a fork, and tasted what was inside. Then she put the lid back on. Next she bent down and opened a big door that was under the pot. A blast of heat came out that scared Hobo, but the scent it carried was delicious. It was the first time that Hobo had ever gotten this close to cooked meat before. Hobo's mouth watered. He knew that he wanted to eat whatever that was.

The woman took out the meat and closed the oven door. Hobo crept out from under the kitchen table. The woman put the meat dish on the counter top and lifted the pot of boiling water off the stove. She turned to drain the water off in the sink. She moved quickly. She stepped on Hobo's tail. He yelped. She screamed. The pot of boiling water and cooked peas spilled onto the floor. Hobo dashed under the table. Hot peas and boiling water splashed in all directions.

"One of them's out!" the woman shouted as she left the kitchen. "Mrs. Billingswort, one of them pups is out and the dinner's ruined!"

Hobo sat there, terrified, under the table. His fur had

protected him from the splashing peas and boiling water, but it hadn't protected him from the woman's foot. She was a heavy woman and his tail hurt. He wasn't cold, but he was shaking all over. Then he noticed that one of the peas was right in front of his nose. He sniffed at it. It didn't smell so bad. He licked it. It tasted pretty good. He stopped shaking. He put his paw on it. It squished. He tasted it again. It was better squished. He ate it all. Then he ate another one. He was about to eat a third when Mrs. Billingswort and the cook returned. Hobo scooted under the table again. The cook was talking.

"I told you more than once, Mrs. Billingswort, that I will not cook with those pups underfoot. It's bad enough having that box in the kitchen."

"Now, Dora, this is the first time they've gotten out . . ."

"And look at the mess! Peas all over the place!"

"My goodness, the poor puppy! Did you scald it with the water?"

"Poor puppy!!! It scared me half to death. I stepped on it and jumped a mile. Lucky for you I didn't fall and break my hip. That's what I should have done. My boyfriend, the one that works for the insurance company, he says a broken hip is worth about twenty thousand dollars, maybe more with complications."

Mrs. Billingswort wasn't listening. She was down on her hands and knees looking for Hobo and calling in a sweet voice, "Puppy? Poor puppy, where are you?"

She saw Hobo right away under the table and gently picked him up. "You poor little thing. Did Dora really step on you? You seem to be all right, though."

She carried him back to the box and put him down

among his brothers and sisters. After that he was Mrs. Billingswort's favorite. She would show him off to her friends and tell them that he was the first to get out of the box. Dora, however, was not pleased. She threatened to either quit or break her hip if the box was not removed from her kitchen. The whole litter of pups was then moved to a corner of Mrs. Billingswort's bedroom. The corner was fenced off with high screens and newspaper was put down. The box was gone. Hobo couldn't get out and his mother couldn't get in. Hobo didn't like this arrangement at all. Neither did Mr. Billingswort when he came home from the office that evening.

"It's time to put an ad in the paper. I'm not going to have my bedroom turned into a zoo."

"They're not weaned yet," said Mrs. Billingswort. "As soon as they're weaned, I promise I'll give them away. But they are Lucy's pups and I want to make sure they find good homes."

"I know how you feel about giving Lucy her chance to have puppies. But we had talked of a pedigreed mate, not some mongrel off the street. I insist that as soon as possible she must be spayed. We can't go through this again in a city apartment."

"I promise. It will only be a week or so before the pups are gone. They're ready for solid food now."

Hobo's mother, Lucy, was allowed to spend the night with the pups. But during the day she was kept out, and instead of a mother, there was a bowl of brown mush in the pen. Hobo sniffed at it. It didn't smell like that meat that came out of the oven, but on the other hand, it didn't smell too badly either. Remembering the pea, he thought maybe squishing it with his paw might improve the flavor. It didn't. It just made a mess. It stuck to his paw and wherever he put it down, it left a little brown mush mark. He licked his paw to get it clean. The mush tasted pretty good. He walked over to the bowl and lapped up some more of it. There were a few chunky bits. These were the best. He ate most of what was in the bowl. His tummy was so full it almost touched the floor. None of his brothers or sisters ate any of the mush the first day. They spent their time lined up against the screen, crying for their mother. But, then, they had never had the experience of doing battle with a bunch of hot peas under the kitchen table. Hobo was pretty proud of himself. He was the first to be weaned. He was growing up.

After a week or so all the puppies were weaned. Mrs. Billingswort put an ad in the paper that read: "FREE . . . Adorable shaggy mixed breed pups looking for good homes." Pretty soon the telephone started ringing. It was a Saturday. Mr. Billingswort said that he wasn't going to sit around and have a bunch of total strangers traipsing through the apartment. So he went to a movie. A number of people came and picked up the pups and put them down and picked them up again. Hobo and the rest of the litter were all feeling pretty mauled over. A couple of his brothers and sisters had been taken away when a young man and woman came. The woman picked up Hobo and held him against her cheek. She called him a little fluff ball. His tummy was full of mush again. Then she held him very close in front of her face and smiled. "That's it! I'm going to call you Fluffy!" That's how Hobo got his first name.

Since Mrs. Billingswort was a person with a great many

shoes, she had prepared shoe boxes with shredded paper in them so the people could carry the puppies safely home. As she put Hobo in the box she said, "Please take good care of him. He's my favorite." The man and woman, whose names were Larry and Gail, promised that they would. Just as they were leaving, Larry asked Mrs. Billingswort if she knew what kind of mixed breed the puppies were. Mrs. Billingswort smiled in a teasing way and said, "He's a genuine Heinz."

"A Heinz?" asked Larry.

"Yes, you know, fifty-seven varieties," said Mrs. Billingswort, laughing. Larry was not amused.

Larry and Gail were newly married. They lived in a small apartment. There was a bedroom, a living/dining room, and a tiny kitchen. Gail called it a kitchenette. It was really just a corner of the living room separated by a counter. Although the apartment was small, it was beautifully furnished with their new wedding presents. Everything smelled like it was still in a store. They bought a little food bowl and a water bowl and a collar and leash. They all smelled of store too. Gail put newspapers down on the kitchenette floor and then put the food and water bowls on top of the newspapers. Even though he had already eaten today, Hobo ate most of the brown mush in the bowl, washed it down with a few laps of water, and trotted out to explore his new home.

There was a beautiful rug in the living room, made of many colors and patterns. Larry called it Oriental and was worried that the puppy might spot it. Hobo didn't know what that meant. Gail said that she thought that he was paper-trained. Hobo didn't know what that meant either.

And, furthermore, he didn't care. He was too interested in all the new sights and smells. There was a sofa, two chairs, and a coffee table in the middle of the living room. The room was small so they were close together and covered most of the Oriental rug. There was a bookcase along the wall. It had a few books in it and a number of the smaller wedding presents. The bedroom didn't have much in it except a bed and a couple of bureaus. They all matched. Gail called it their bedroom suite. There was a closet in the bedroom too. The closet door was closed, but there were interesting smells from there, leathery smells, like shoes. Hobo wished he could get in.

Hobo's favorite place was the sofa or, rather, under the sofa. There was just enough room to crawl in. It was dark and cozy. He felt very safe there. It was like his own personal lair. He could go under the two chairs and the bed and the coffee table too, but none of them felt as good and safe as being under the sofa.

Since Larry and Gail didn't have a dining room, they ate off the coffee table. This was lower than any other table Hobo had ever seen. The aroma of food was much stronger. He always hung around the table when they ate. Gail would give him little tidbits from her plate. Larry objected, saying that it was bad training, but Gail continued to do it anyhow. Hobo began to get the feeling that Larry didn't like him. Particularly after he had spotted the Oriental rug a few times.

Since both Larry and Gail worked, Hobo was left alone in the apartment all day long. It was boring there by himself. He wished he had his brothers and sisters to play with. He also had this very strong need to chew . . . he didn't know why. It was just something to do and it felt good. He roamed the apartment looking for something to chew. In the bedroom he discovered that, for the first time, the closet door was open. It was dark in there. Cautiously he crept in. There were clothes hanging up that didn't interest him, but on the floor of the closet there were a number of pairs of shoes. There was a pair of Gail's shoes that had an interesting smell, but there was too much plastic in them. Over in the darkest corner he got the strong scent of leather, real leather. It was one of Larry's loafers. He sniffed all over it. It was delicious. He sunk his little baby teeth into the leather and shook his head fiercely. The shoe was heavy. It hurt his neck but it felt so good on his teeth. He let go of the shoe and stalked it. Then he pounced again, sunk his teeth into it, and pulled and shook. He growled a savage puppy growl as he worked the shoe over toward the open closet door. Triumphantly he wrestled the shoe into the bedroom. He was exhausted and dropped it. He circled it, panting and barking at the same time. He got very excited by the idea of attacking this giant shoe. He worked himself up into a frenzy. He pounced on it again. It felt so good to sink his teeth into that leather. He shook it and tugged at it until he had wrestled it under the bed. Now he had it in a safe place where he could chew on it to his heart's content.

When Larry found out there was a terrible scene. He threatened to take Hobo back. Gail cried and Hobo found himself penned in the kitchenette the next day with a big rubber bone to chew on. The rubber bone had a funny smell to it. Hobo gave it a few licks and sunk his teeth into it a couple of times, but it wasn't like a real bone or even like real leather. He decided to try and find a way over the window screen that Larry had put between the kitchenette and the living room. Hobo tried jumping over it, but even though he was a very good jumper, it was too high. He tried chewing a hole in it, but it was flat and he couldn't get his teeth into it. There was a wooden frame all around it. He got a hold of that with his teeth and pulled. It moved. It was the kind of screen that slides on itself to fit all kinds of windows. He pulled on it again and again. Finally, he pulled it loose from where Larry had wedged it with the garbage can. It fell on Hobo. He gave a yelp and scrambled out from under it. He stood there for a moment, watching the fallen screen. It didn't move and neither did Hobo. He didn't trust it. It had attacked him once and he wasn't certain that it wouldn't come at him again. Very stealthily he worked his way over to it and sniffed at it. It smelled of wood and aluminum. There was nothing too threatening about that. He looked up. On the other side of the flattened screen was the whole rest of the apartment. All he had to do was walk over that screen and he'd be free. He wanted to do that very much. But if he stepped on the screen, it might rise up and attack him again. He didn't want that to happen. He sniffed at it thoroughly. He barked and growled to show it who was boss. Then, very carefully, he put his paw on it. Nothing happened. He screwed his courage up to the sticking point and jumped. He cleared the screen in two bounds and was in the living room.

Hobo walked around, savoring his victory over the screen. Suddenly, the need to chew was overwhelming. He went into the bedroom. The closet was closed. If he couldn't get at the shoes, nothing else in the bedroom interested him. He had to find something to chew on. He wandered around the living room, sniffing at different objects. Finally, he settled for a book. It was a thin book, full of pictures of old-fashioned automobiles. Larry had shown it to a friend the night before. The friend had called it a coffee table book and told him that he shouldn't hide it in the bookcase. "It's a prestige book," his friend had said. So Larry left it on the coffee table. One corner was sticking out over the edge.

Hobo discovered that by standing on his hind legs and stretching he could just reach that corner of the book. He sniffed it. It smelled of cloth and cardboard and glue. The glue was the best. He licked it. That was it. He had to have that book! He sunk his teeth into the cover. The book was thin enough for him to get his mouth over it. The cardboard felt good on his teeth, just enough resistance, almost like leather, and the glue tasted delicious. He pulled at the book, but it hardly moved. He pulled again and a piece of the corner came off. He barked at it and jumped up at it, but he couldn't get a good enough grip on it to pull it down. The contest was unfair. He could never win, attacking from the floor. He had to get up there on that table. He jumped and caught his paws on the shiny edge of the table, but it was too slippery. He fell back down. He tried jumping up on the sofa. His claws caught in the fabric and he scrambled up. He was on the sofa! Boy! It was terrific up there on the sofa! The cushions were soft and bouncy. He pounced around on the sofa for a while, until that need to chew came back to him . . .

Hobo looked over at the book on the coffee table. It wasn't so far away, maybe about the length of Larry's loafer. He went over to the edge of the sofa and examined the distance between where he was and where the book was, over on the coffee table. Maybe it was a little more than a foot, but he thought he could make it. Then he looked down. It seemed a long way down to the Oriental rug. For the second time that day he screwed up his courage and jumped. He landed on the coffee table and slid across its shiny surface until he almost fell off the other side. He backed up quickly. The coffee table was not like the sofa. It was very slippery underfoot. However, it was full of good smells from the various meals that Gail and Larry had eaten on it. There were even a few toast crumbs left over from breakfast. He ate them. He sniffed around to see if there were any more. Instead, he encountered the book. There it was, lying in wait for him. He growled an eager puppy growl. The book didn't do anything. He stood back and barked at it. Still the book didn't do anything. He pounced on it, got a good grip on a corner of it, and shook. The book slid a little. Hobo backed off and pounced again with full puppy force. The book slid off the table and Hobo slid off with it. They both crashed to the rug below. The cover of the book flipped over and hit Hobo. He jumped back, growled, and attacked. The book was a sneaky fighter. Hobo grabbed the cover and pulled. The book moved. He had a plan now. He would pull the wounded book back into his lair under the sofa and chew it up at his leisure. He shook and tugged until it was far under the sofa. He was exhausted from his battle. He curled up and fell asleep next to his defeated enemy.

Gail came home first and saw that the screen was knocked down. "Fluff! Here, Fluff!" she called. He darted out from under the sofa. She scooped him up in her arms. "Fluffy, how did you get out?" She carried him into the living room. "Have you been good? No spots on Larry's rug? Oh, Fluff, how could you! Bad dog!" She carried him back to the kitchenette, put up the screen, and took out a can of rug cleaner. She worked over the spot he had made on the rug and was just returning the cleaner when Larry came in. Before he could say anything, Gail said cheerfully, "Hi, honey. You've got to put up a better gate. Fluffy got out. But he didn't get into anything and there was only one small spot. I just cleaned it up."

Larry looked at the paper on the kitchen floor. "Maybe he needs to go to a dog psychiatrist. He always goes on the rug, *never* on the paper! There must be something wrong with him!"

"It takes a little time and patience, Larry." Gail kissed him. "Maybe he's ready. Why don't you take him for a walk? I'll fix us something to eat while you two are out."

"I don't know why I bother," said Larry, as he clipped the leash on Hobo's collar. "He never does anything when I walk him. The closest he ever came was in the elevator."

"It's the routine that counts. He'll get the idea one of these days. Good luck!"

Larry and Hobo went down on the elevator, out through the lobby, and into the street. The street was a very interesting place, but Hobo hated the leash. Just when he'd find something he'd like to sniff, Larry would drag him away. Other times, when there was absolutely nothing worth sniffing, Larry would make him sit there forever, while he'd say things like, "Come on, boy, do your stuff." Or, "You can do it. I know you've got it in you." Or, with a touch of anger, "Fluff, just do it!" Hobo would wag his tail to try to cheer Larry up, but it never worked. Finally, in a bad mood, Larry would drag him back into the building.

On this particular evening, one of their neighbors, a woman in a tennis outfit, came in with them. She looked down at Hobo and said, "He's adorable." Then she patted him. Larry smiled a kind of fishy smile and said, "Yeah, he is kind of cute, I guess." The building had two sets of elevators. Larry and Gail lived on one side. The tennis lady lived on the other. She and Larry wanted to talk for a while in the lobby, so she rested her tennis racket up against the wall. Hobo sniffed the wooden racket. It was kind of a special smell. He liked it.

The lady looked down and said rather loudly, "For God's sake, Larry! Look what your dog is doing!" Larry yanked on the leash so hard that Hobo was jerked off the ground. It choked him so hard he couldn't breathe. It also hurt his neck. Larry was scolding him and apologizing to the lady at the same time. She was so angry she just walked away. Hobo decided that he would never go again while the leash was on. That must be why Larry was so angry. Even if he had to go very badly, he would try never to go when he and Larry were out for a walk. Maybe that would make Larry happy.

When they got to the apartment, Gail asked cheerfully how it went. "*It* went in the lobby!" Larry replied in an angry voice. "It *went* right on Linda Kuppleman's tennis racket! I was never so embarrassed in my life."

"Let's sit down and relax, Larry," said Gail. She led him into the living room and they sat down on the sofa.

"Where did he do it this time?" said Larry sullenly, looking at the rug.

"You can't see it, can you? It was only a little one. I cleaned it up."

"I can see it. Right over there." Larry pointed to where Hobo had spotted the rug. "We might as well face it. The rug's ruined. Great Uncle Omar's priceless heirloom is now a worthless wreck, thanks to that miserable mutt."

"Larry!" Gail was shocked. "Don't be so down. Old rugs like this were made for shieks' tents. Camels, goats, and who knows what have probably been on this rug, and it's survived, beautifully."

"Yeah, until dear little Fluffy got a hold of it."

"Oh, Larry, come on. Once he's trained, we'll send it out to the cleaners and that will be the end of it."

"You mean the end of our bank account. Do you know what it costs to clean a fine old Oriental rug like this?" Larry didn't wait for Gail's answer. A new concern came to his mind. "Gail! Where did you put my *Great Cars of the Teens and Twenties* book?!"

"I didn't put it anyplace."

"It was right here on the coffee table last night. Remember, we were looking at it. And I'm sure it was here at breakfast too. You must have moved it."

"Larry, I didn't touch it. I know how you are about things like that."

"Well, it couldn't just walk off by itself!" Larry was getting very upset.

"Larry, don't get upset. I'll bet you put it in the bookcase."

"Gail, it's a coffee table book! It's a book to show off! Why would I put it in the bookcase?" Larry got up to look in the bookcase.

Gail had put some cheese dip and crackers on the table. Hobo had been sitting on the rug, wagging his tail and waiting. The aroma of the cheese was making his mouth water. He decided to show off his new trick. Maybe that would make Larry and Gail feel better. He scrambled up onto the sofa, jumped over to the coffee table, and snatched a piece of cheese. Then he wagged his tail.

"Fluffy! No!" Gail was surprised.

"That's it! The little monster snitched my book!" Larry tried to grab Hobo from the side of the sofa. He missed, but he managed to knock the dip over. It made a big spot on Uncle Omar's Oriental rug. Gail screamed. Hobo dashed under a chair. He wished he could get under the sofa, but both Larry and Gail were in the way. Gail looked down at Larry on his hands and knees. With cool contempt she said, "I don't think Fluffy took your stupid book at all. You just can't remember where you put it."

Larry tried to grab Hobo under the chair.

"This is *not* attractive, Larry. Your hostility is showing."

Hobo dashed from under one chair to the other. Larry lunged after him. Since Larry was large and the room was small, with the furniture quite close together, he knocked over the coffee table, sending everything onto Uncle Omar's Oriental rug.

Gail screamed, "Stop this right now! You are out of control!"

"Shut up!" Larry yelled. "Help me catch the mutt."

"Don't you speak to me like that! And don't you dare harm that defenseless little puppy!" Gail was furious.

Hobo dashed under the sofa. Larry, still on the floor, reached his arm in after him. He didn't catch Hobo, but he did get hold of the chewed-up book. He stood up and shoved the book under Gail's nose. He was shaking all over.

"Defenseless little puppy, eh? That's thirty-nine dollars and ninety-nine cents, down the drain! Plus my loafers, that's another forty bucks! Eighty dollars in two days! Not to mention the rug! Who knows what he'll destroy tomorrow? I don't want to see him here tomorrow. Tomorrow, you get rid of this termite, and I don't care how!" Larry was still shaking with anger. Gail was shaking with tears. And Hobo was shaking with fear, even though he was still safe in his lair under the sofa.

The next day Gail took Hobo to a place where unwanted cats and dogs are put up for adoption. It was called an animal shelter. She cried when she gave him to the volunteer lady attendant. The lady told Gail that because there were so many stray animals in the city, if nobody adopted him within three days he would have to be destroyed. "I love him, but we just can't keep him," Gail said. Then she gave Hobo a kiss and left quickly.

SECOND NAME, "BOUNCE"

SO FAR IN HOBO'S YOUNG LIFE, HE HAD ONLY experienced people's apartments. The animal shelter was a whole new scene. And he didn't like it at all. For starters he didn't like being in a cage. He longed to be free. He tried to find a way to pull it open and knock down a side, like he had done to the screen that Larry had put up to keep him in the kitchenette. But this cage was made of very heavy wire all around. It was made so you couldn't get out. Then there was the smell. It wasn't really a bad smell. It just wasn't a very interesting smell. It was a clean, antiseptic kind of scent. The worst thing about it was that it was constantly there, and that took all the pleasure out of using your nose. Then there were all the other dogs in all the other cages. Hobo had never seen so many dogs. Most of them were tiny puppies that had just been weaned. All together they made a lot of noise. Some of them were always yapping. Some of them were always whining. And there were always a few of them growling at each other in play. Hobo was beyond all that now. He wasn't a tiny puppy. Their noisy carrying-on seemed a bit silly to him. A few of his cage mates were older dogs. They looked tired and miserable and they all lay in their cages and waited. They never made any noise at all. Nobody who came in looking for a pet paid much attention to them. Hobo was quite unique. He was the only middle-aged puppy in the place. After a while he began to wonder why he was there. Why were they all there? Even though life with Larry and Gail had its ups and downs, it was better than being in a cage. Maybe Gail would come back for him. He didn't know what to think. One thing he was sure of, he liked people and their apartments better than the cages in this temporary dog hotel.

Hobo spent two days at the animal shelter. Not many people came. But whenever somebody did come, Hobo would jump up against the cage door, bark, and wag his tail and try to make friends. The third day was a Saturday and, being a weekend, more people came to the shelter looking for a pet to adopt. Among them were Allan and Marsha. They looked somewhat older than Larry and Gail. Hobo could tell, right away, that Marsha liked him.

"Allan! Over here. How about this one? He's so lively and full of bounce. And he's not a tiny puppy like so many of them. I bet he could hold his own with Toby."

Allan came over and looked in the cage at Hobo. Hobo jumped up against the cage door, wagged his tail furiously, and made small whimpering noises that went right to Marsha's heart.

"Oh, you poor little dear." She put her finger through the cage and Hobo licked it. "Yes, you're a sweetie pie. You like my finger, don't you. Allan, get the attendant. Let's take a better look at this one."

Allan came back with the attendant, who opened Hobo's cage. Nobody had to reach in and get him. He came out like a cannonball and leaped into Marsha's arms. He was all over her in a second, licking her face and nuzzling her ear. She laughed with delight. Allan took Hobo from Marsha and held him. He asked the attendant how old he was and whether he was housebroken.

"I can't say, for sure. We don't get much background on them, you know. I'd say he was probably about three months old. At that age he should be paper-trained, anyhow."

"Oh, Allan, he's perfect. He's big enough to take care of himself, you know, with Toby. And yet he's still a puppy."

"It's a birthday present for our son. He's just five," Allan explained to the attendant.

"They should be just about a match for each other. If you want to take him, there are a few forms to fill out." The attendant gave Marsha the leash that Gail had left with Hobo and she clipped it to his collar. While Allan filled out the forms, Marsha and Hobo walked around the lobby of the shelter looking at some kittens in a large glass cage. Hobo kept jumping up at the cage and barking. She called him away from the kittens and held out her arms. He jumped right into them. Allan finished the forms and met them by the door.

"I've got the perfect name for him. I've never seen a puppy with so much bounce as this one. Just look." She put him down and then held out her arms. "Here, Bounce," she called. Hobo jumped into her arms again. "Isn't that a perfect name for him, Bounce?"

"It's different, I'll give you that," said Allan, mulling it over in his mind. "Yes. I guess Bounce is a pretty good name for him."

"Pretty good? It's terrific! It's just right and Toby's going to love it."

"Bounce sure is a funny name," said Toby, when they brought his birthday present home. "Did he already have it or did you make it up?"

"Your mother made it up, son."

"Don't you like it, Toby? You'll find he's full of it—bounce, I mean."

Toby picked Hobo up and held him as high as he could. Then he dropped him. Hobo landed flat on all fours, yelped as he hit, and darted under the sofa.

"He didn't bounce! You said he would bounce!" Toby was being difficult. It wasn't for nothing that relatives nicknamed him Toby the Terror.

"Toby! He's a puppy, not a ball. I said he was full of bounce, meaning full of energy," his mother explained. "You mustn't drop him like that. You could hurt him and then he won't like you."

"He doesn't anyway. I dropped him 'cause he was going to go on me."

Marsha looked at her son with curious surprise. "Toby, what makes you say that?"

"Son, Bounce is a special present for your fifth birthday. Your mother and I thought you would like a pet of your own. You're old enough now to take care of him. You can have fun feeding him and training him to be a good dog."

"Some birthday present. It sounds like a lot of work."

Marsha was coaxing Hobo out from under the sofa with friendly words. Hobo responded and she cradled him in her arms. "Let's all sit down on the sofa so he can get to know us." Allan and Marsha sat down. Toby stood in front of them studying Hobo, trying to figure out, with his five-year-old head, whether this dog was going to be fun to have around or trouble. Marsha was petting Hobo and scratching him behind his ears, which he enjoyed. "You see, Toby, if you are nice to him, he'll be nice to you. Why don't you hold him and pet him?" She started to hand Hobo over to Toby, but the boy backed off.

"What's the matter? Don't you want to hold him?"

"It's no fun just scratching him."

"Don't you like your present, son?"

"He's all right, I guess. But if I hold him for long, he'll go on me."

"He doesn't do it on me," Marsha said.

"Well, he will on me."

"Son, one of the big things that you must do for your dog is to train him so that he knows where to go and when. Now the woman at the shelter thinks that he should be paper-trained by now. Come, I'll help you. We'll put down some newspapers in a corner of the kitchen so that he knows where he's supposed to go. And if he makes a mistake, then it'll be your job to carry him, right away, over to the paper so that he'll get the idea."

"He'll go on me."

"He won't go on you. I don't know where you got such a silly idea." Allan put down newspapers in a corner of the kitchen. He also put down food and water bowls that they had just bought. Toby watched his father do these things with a very bored expression on his face. From the pet store paper bag that held the two bowls, Allan took out a rubber bone. "Here, you'll have fun with this, Toby. It's a chew bone. Puppies need to chew a lot to make their teeth grow. Let's see how he likes it. Put him down, Marsha."

Marsha, who was still holding Hobo, put him on the floor. Allan called him over and wriggled the rubber bone in front of him. Hobo pounced on it and sunk his teeth into it and shook. Allan shook the other end. "Here, son, you take it and play with him."

"Naw," said Toby, turning away.

"Why not?" said his father, down on his hands and knees. "It's fun."

"He'll bite me."

"Toby," said Marsha, "he won't bite you. See, he's not biting Daddy. He's biting the bone."

Allan, leaving the rubber bone on the floor, stood up. "You're not afraid of this little puppy, are you, a big five-year-old boy, like you?"

"Naw. I just don't feel like playing with him now. I'm going to watch TV." Toby went into his room and turned on his set. It was a color set. It was his big birthday present last year. A rerun of "Star Trek" was on.

Allan looked at Marsha. "What do you think?"

"I think it's going to be just fine. But maybe we shouldn't press too much about the training and feeding right away. Let's let them get to know each other first."

"But, Marsha, that was the whole point, to give Toby some responsibility, make a man out of him. He needs that."

"Allan, he's only five!"

"When I was five, I had to care for a flock of twelve chickens."

"I know, I know. But Toby's growing up in a city. Things are different. I agree he should have the experience of caring for a dog, but I don't think we should lay it on him all at once."

Allan didn't say anything.

Hobo had become bored with chewing on a rubber bone that just lay there on the floor. It tasted and smelled exactly like the other rubber bone that Larry and Gail had bought. It was only fun to chew if someone was on the other end wiggling it. Allan and Marsha were sitting on the sofa reading the newspaper. Hobo jumped up on the sofa, squirmed under the newspaper, and settled into Marsha's lap. She looked at Allan. "He's a cutie, isn't he?" Allan mumbled something in vague agreement and continued to read.

Both Allan and Marsha worked full time. Allan was a computer programmer for a large insurance company. Everything he put into the computer came out just the way he planned it. He liked things that happened that way. Marsha worked for a TV game show. She was a production assistant. Her job was to prepare the contestants before the show, tell them where to stand, which cues to look for, and what to do. However, since the contestants had to be in the studio two hours before the show was taped, Marsha's main job was to keep them from getting so nervous that they couldn't go on. She was very good at this.

Most of the money that Marsha made went to pay Mrs. Patterson to take care of the apartment and Toby. Mrs. Patterson had been hired as a mother's helper. The thing she liked best about her job was the color television. She spent most of her day sitting on the sofa with a can of soda in her hand, watching the flickering images that came up on the big color screen. When she straightened out the bedroom, she watched the smaller set in there. When she made Toby's bed and hung his pajamas up, she watched whatever he was watching. Since the kitchen didn't have a set, she spent as little time in there as possible.

She and Toby had a secret agreement. As long as he didn't make trouble for her, she would let him do whatever he wanted in his own room. The result was that Toby's room was always a complete mess, which was the way he liked it, while the rest of the apartment remained reasonably calm and neat, which was the way Mrs. Patterson liked it. In this way they had as little contact with each other as possible, which was the way they both liked it. Mrs. Patterson was not too happy to see Hobo in the apartment that first Monday morning. She sensed this small furry creature was going to upset their arrangement. Marsha was just leaving the apartment for the TV studio and was hastily explaining about the birthday present. She suggested that Mrs. Patterson take the puppy out with her when she took Toby to the playground in the afternoon.

As soon as Marsha left, Mrs. Patterson popped herself a can of soda and settled down on the sofa. As she turned on the tube she called out to make sure Toby was in his room. She could hear the cartoon sound effects, so she knew his set was on, but that was no guarantee that he was there.

She called again. Finally, Toby mumbled an answer and Mrs. Patterson turned up "The Gong Show." She had just settled down on the sofa when Hobo scampered over and jumped up into her lap. "Hey, you! Down!" she commanded. At the same time she swept him off her lap. Hobo rolled onto the floor. He wasn't hurt, so he jumped up again. He liked laps. This time Mrs. Patterson picked him up by the scruff of his neck and put him on the floor. "You stay there, puppy!" she said loudly, shaking her finger at him.

Hobo looked up at her and cocked his head. She paid him no attention. She was riveted to the set, watching a ventriloquist perform who used a real person for the dummy. Hobo sat there for a moment, studying the situation. He wanted to get up on her lap, but he was pretty sure that jumping wasn't the way to do it. He decided to bark in a friendly fashion and wag his tail. Most people seemed to like that. However, Mrs. Patterson shook her finger at him again and said rather loudly, "You shut up, puppy!" Hobo cocked his head at her and barked again, all the time wagging his tail. Mrs. Patterson looked down at him. "Okay, okay, if I pick you up, you better be quiet." She reached down and plopped him in her lap. Hobo snuggled in and promptly went to sleep. They spent a very agreeable morning together in this way.

Every day Mrs. Patterson made a peanut butter and jelly sandwich for Toby. He was supposed to have a glass of milk with it, but again, they had worked out a secret agreement. Toby hated milk and threw a tantrum when she first tried to force him to drink it. Mrs. Patterson hated tantrums and trouble of all kinds, so she decided to let Toby have the

Coke that he wanted. After lunch, if it wasn't raining, Mrs. Patterson took Toby to a playground in the park nearby. On this day she had to take Hobo also.

Mrs. Patterson snapped the leash on Hobo's collar. Toby straddled his big wheels bike. All together they headed for the park. Mrs. Patterson kept up a steady pace along the way. This was a great frustration for Hobo. So many interesting smells were passed by with hardly a sniff. Hobo tried putting on the brakes a couple of times when there was something he particularly wanted to savor, but it was useless. He was no match for Mrs. Patterson's constant, heavy tug.

The park was a new experience. It was the first time that Hobo had ever encountered dirt, grass, and trees. They were wonderful, marvelous things. Then there was a squirrel. Something deep inside of him told Hobo to chase it. He tried, but the end of the leash came very quickly. He flipped up into the air and over on his back. He had to get his feet under him quickly or be dragged along by Mrs. Patterson. He hated that leash! Finally, they came to a bench. Mrs. Patterson hooked the loop end of the leash over a knob on the bench and started to read a paperback book.

Toby saw Bruce over by the swings. Bruce was his regular friend at the playground. Bruce was going to be five himself in a few weeks.

Although the length of the leash limited how far he could go, Hobo could explore that area to his heart's content. He was fascinated with dirt. It felt good to scratch in it. And when he did it turned up new scents only hinted at on the surface. He worked his front paws quickly, throwing the dirt behind him. Digging down, he discovered an earthworm that slithered away and a big, black beetle with pincers that got hold of his nose. He shook his head sharply and the beetle went flying. He continued to dig himself out a hollow place in the dirt. He had just turned around a few times to make sure he could sleep in it when Toby, Bruce, and Bruce's older brother, Mike, arrived. Mike was eight. He bent down and started to pet Hobo.

"Hi, ya, fella. What's your name?"

"Bounce," said Toby.

"Bounce?"

"Yeah. My mother made it up. Pretty stupid, huh?"

"Yeah, maybe. But he's nice and friendly anyhow." Hobo was licking Mike's fingers. Bruce started petting him too.

"You're sure lucky to have a dog all your own." Bruce was jealous.

"Bet it's not really his," said Mike. "Nobody'd be dumb enough to give Toby a live animal for a pet."

"He is too mine! He's my birthday present." Toby took the leash off the knob and dragged Hobo away. "Come on, maybe I'll let you play with him."

Mrs. Patterson looked up from her paperback book long enough to call after him, "You be careful!" Toby didn't bother to answer.

"What can you play with him?" asked Bruce, as they approached the playground slide.

"Lots of things," said Toby, putting his mischievous mind into high gear. "Hold him a minute." He gave the leash to Bruce and climbed up the ladder on the back of the slide. "Hand him up," commanded Toby. Since Mike was taller, he handed Hobo up to Toby.

"Have you done this before?" questioned Mike.

"Sure. He loves it," said Toby, grabbing Hobo from Mike's outstretched arms. "You catch him at the bottom."

Toby placed Hobo headfirst on the slippery metal slide. Hobo was terrified. It was such a long way from where he was to where Mike and Bruce were at the bottom. He tried to scramble back up, but Toby held him firmly in position. "Okay, are you guys ready?"

"Sure," said Mike.

"Bombs away!" shouted Toby as he let go of Hobo with a downward shove.

Hobo tried to stop by digging his claws into the shiny metal surface of the slide. But that seemed to make him go faster. He tried to turn around and go back up. He started running as fast as his feet could go. But no matter how fast he ran up, he kept sliding down. Bruce and Mike were laughing as they grabbed him at the bottom. Hobo's feet were still churning away as they picked him up.

"See. What'd I tell you," said Toby pompously. "He's my dog. I can do whatever I want with him."

"Then do it again," said Mike. "Only start him backside down. It's fun to see his little feet try to run up while he slides down."

And so they played Bombs Away a few more times until Toby got a better idea. After the last slide, Toby said, "Bring him over to the baby swings and I'll really show you how to play Bombs Away."

The baby swings were set on a rubber-coated base sur-

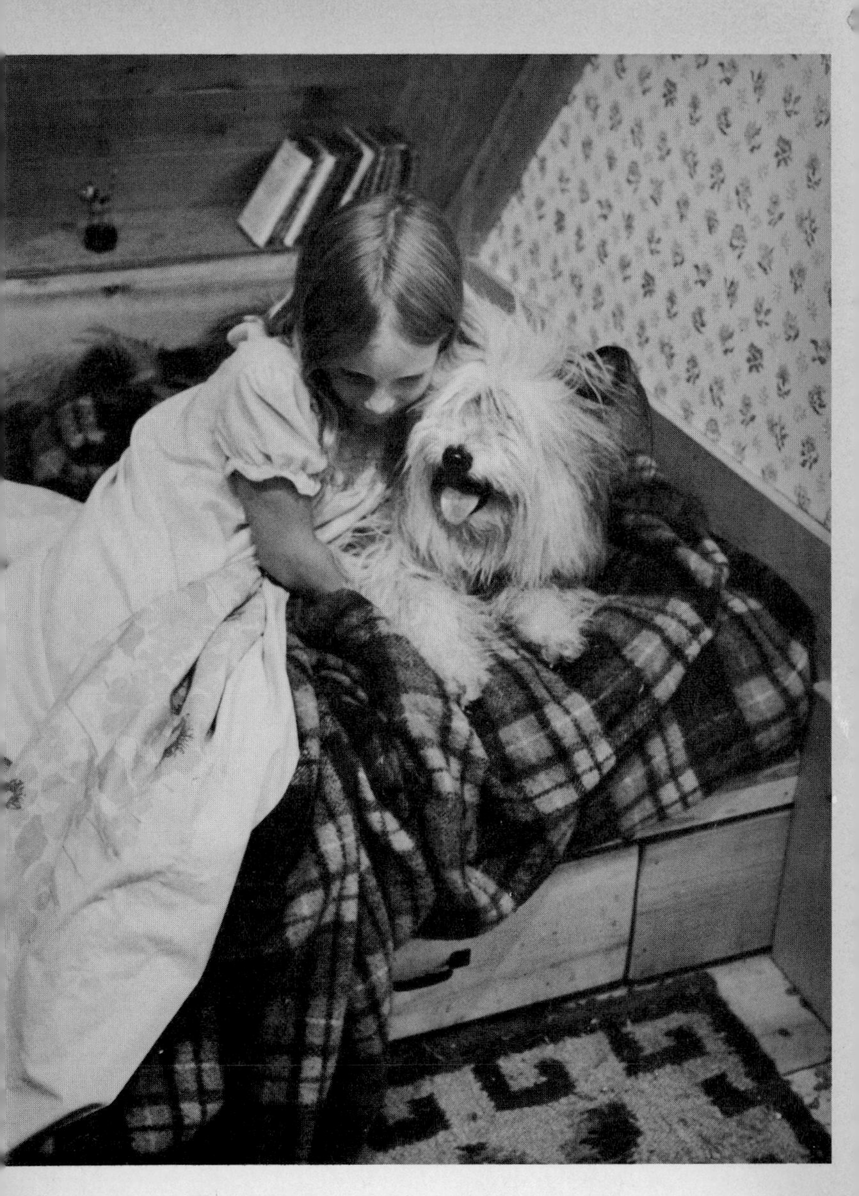

"Silly old Shag, you're a dog not a bird."

Up on the roof Hobo is safe from Bruno.

Stranded on the highway—how can Hobo get across?

Toby "dresses up" Hobo.

"Catch him!"

Hobo poses for Alice in his favorite chair.

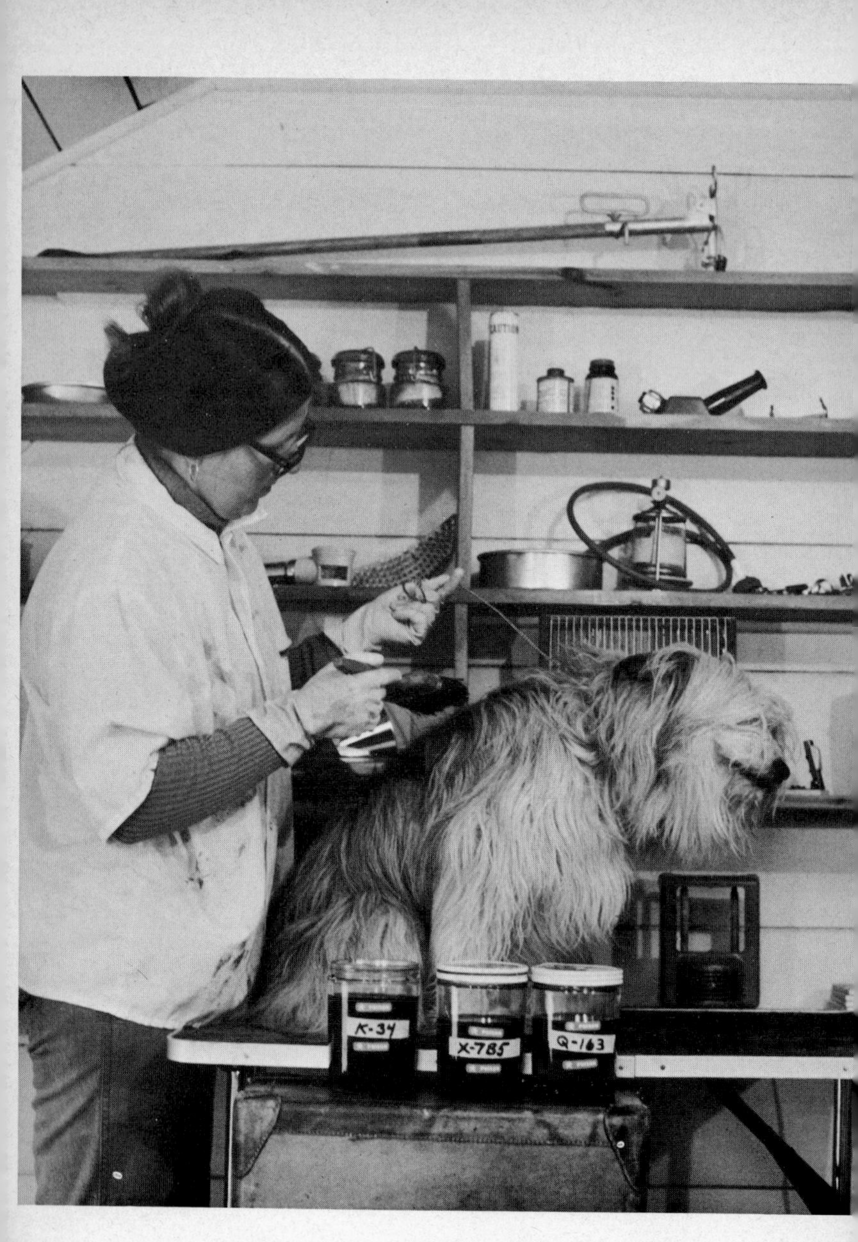

“You’re not going to give me any trouble, are you?”

ESCAPE!

Home at last!

rounded by a deep sand pit. The swings were like little chairs with no legs. They had a safety bar that slid down in front. They were made for toddlers, so Toby has a tight squeeze getting into the seat, but he knew he couldn't manage Hobo with him on the regular swings. Once he was in and the front bar down, he told Mike to hand him the puppy, which he did.

"Gee, Toby, I didn't know you still played on the baby swings."

"Shut up, Mike. And give me a push."

Mike gave him a number of pushes, sending Toby and Hobo about as high as the swing would go. At the peak of the ride Toby shouted, "Bombs Away!" and tossed Hobo out of the chair. Hobo used every muscle in his body, including his tail, to keep his feet under him. For a moment, there was a strangely pleasurable sensation as he seemed to float in the air. The loop end of his leash drifted by as if it were flying along all by itself. Then, suddenly, he was aware that he was no longer flying. He was falling very fast. With a thud, his feet went deep into the sand. Then his chest hit and knocked the wind out of him, and his leash plopped onto the sand next to him. He shook his head clear and struggled to get out of the deep sand.

Toby was still swinging very high and very fast. He couldn't stop himself. He called out to Mike. "Hey, slow it down. Stop it, Mike! . . . Please!"

Mike just stood there laughing. "What's the matter, Toby, are the baby swings too much for you? Hey, if you want to get off, why don't you do Bombs Away yourself!"

Toby called to Bruce, who was standing by the sand pit, laughing too. "Catch him. Don't let him get away."

But Hobo was already running through the sand as fast as his legs could carry him. Bruce ran after him, but Hobo was faster. Mike now joined the chase and after him came Toby. There was a large concrete play mountain in the middle of the sand pit. It had a sculptured lumpy surface so children could climb over it. It also had two tunnels that went through it and crossed in the middle. Hobo dashed into the nearest tunnel, took a left turn in the middle, came out, and scrambled up to the top of the mountain where he could watch everything going on around him. Bruce, Mike, and Toby dashed into the tunnel and kept on going straight through. When they got out they wondered where the dog was. They looked in all directions. There was no sight of him. Toby was just starting to lay the blame on Bruce for losing him when Mike spotted Hobo on top of the mountain. Two little kids were petting him. "Grab his leash," yelled Toby as the three boys started up the concrete slope.

But Hobo heard Toby's voice and was on his way down the opposite side before the little children could do anything. Hobo ducked into the tunnel again and waited. When the boys came in one entrance, he went out another. The boys finally got smart and each took a separate entrance. But there were only three boys and four entrances. Hobo could always escape. They played this game until Toby got Mrs. Patterson to help. She was reluctant to put down her paperback until she thought of Marsha's reaction if the puppy were lost on the first day out. Marsha liked the little dog. She would be very angry. She might even fire Mrs. Patterson and, all things considered, this was about the easiest job Mrs. Patterson had ever had.

Hobo was by one of the tunnel entrances waiting to see

what the boys and Mrs. Patterson would do. As they approached, he darted into the tunnel. "Block it," ordered Toby. Mrs. Patterson stood in front of the entrance where Hobo had just disappeared. The three boys went into the other entrances and, working their way toward the center, forced Hobo into Mrs. Patterson's waiting arms. She took the leash and marched Hobo back to the bench. "You don't play with him anymore today," decreed Mrs. Patterson to Toby.

"Who'd want him? He's a nuisance," said Toby haughtily as he turned to go back to the playground. Hobo flopped into the dirt nest that he had scratched up, grateful for its cool softness. He was still panting hard. It was good to rest.

That evening when Marsha came home, she asked Mrs. Patterson eagerly, "How did it go with the puppy and Toby?"

"Fine, just fine."

"Did they play together in the park?"

"Oh, yeah. They were fine. Cute puppy."

"Yes. He's a dear. I'm so glad it went well. See you tomorrow."

That evening Hobo stayed close to Marsha. He did allow Toby to pick him up a couple of times, but only when Marsha was near. These times Toby petted him gently and spoke kind words to him. But Hobo didn't trust him. As for Allan, except for a friendly pat once in a while, he pretty much ignored the puppy.

Allan and Marsha's apartment had a kitchen with a door that closed, and the newspapers pretty much covered the entire kitchen floor. Since Hobo was shut in there every night and whenever the family went out, it was pretty easy to become paper-trained. For all practical purposes, Toby had nothing to do with it. His father always changed the newspapers and his mother always filled the food and water bowls. Closed in the kitchen a great deal of the time, Hobo soon became an expert at what a puppy can do in there besides becoming paper-trained. The first thing he discovered was the garbage can. He found it one Saturday afternoon when everyone was out shopping. The can was under the sink. Cabinet doors kept it out of sight, but not out of scent. The aroma from that can was simply delicious. At first Hobo just stood in front of the closed cabinet door and barked. The door didn't open. He jumped up at it a number of times, but it still wouldn't open. He sniffed the crack around the door and started to drool in anticipation of all the good things that were just on the other side. He lay down and studied the situation carefully, cocking his head from one side to the other. He discovered that the door hung over the baseboard at the bottom. He got his paw under it and pulled. The magnetic catch was not as strong as he was. The door popped open and Hobo jumped back in surprise. But only for an instant because there, in front of him, stood the glorious garbage can. He jumped up at the rim of it and knocked it over. All sorts of good things came tumbling out: a steak bone, a frozen orange juice container full of bacon fat (which spilled over the kitchen floor), crusty, stale bread, paper wrappers of all kinds, and, the most fun of all, a milk carton! The milk carton smelled of slightly soured milk. Hobo pounced on it. It skidded through the puddle of bacon fat, picking up added flavor. Hobo put his paw on it and tore off a piece with his teeth. He chewed the goodness out of that piece and tossed it aside. Then he pounced on the milk container again and tore off another piece. Then the steak bone caught his attention and he worked it over. The paper wrappers came next, then back to the milk carton and then to the steak bone. There were too many good things to enjoy. His senses were overwhelmed. He couldn't concentrate on just one thing for any length of time. He was having an orgy of food and fun. But it was exhausting fun. After a while, with his tummy quite full, he turned around and around a number of times to make a nice nest in the garbage and fell asleep.

Hobo was dreaming of the glories of garbage when Allan, Marsha, and Toby came home. Allan was angry. Marsha was shocked and Toby thought it was all very funny. Allan and Marsha cleaned up the mess while Toby went into his room and turned on the TV. Somehow, he was not learning much about responsibility.

The one thing Toby was learning was that the puppy was fun to play with. That first day in the park, when Toby had shown him off to his friends, had proved that the dog could take it. And if he could take it, Toby was the one to dish it out. However, Mrs. Patterson had remained firm about keeping the puppy leashed to her bench, so Toby had to play with him in his room in the morning. This was agreeable to Mrs. Patterson, since both her charges were closed in one room together, making her job that much easier.

For Hobo, however, this latest arrangement was bad news. It wasn't so much being in Toby's room that he minded, it was being with Toby. The room was a marvelous place for a puppy. It was a tangled jungle of wood, plastic, cardboard, paper, and a few leather objects, all suitable for chewing. Trucks, cars, blocks, crayons, a baseball mitt, shoes, construction sets, balls, wheels, rings, books all added up to puppy heaven. Toby was the problem. He treated Hobo like he was some kind of mechanized toy that had no feelings and never ran down. Toby would tie him to a truck or a car in hopes that he would pull it. Instead, Hobo would get hopelessly tangled in the string. Toby would then become bored and return to watching the TV. The set was never turned off. Hobo would have to chew his way out of the tangle.

Another game that Toby liked was Astronaut. He had a toy space helmet that was much too big for him. He would stuff Hobo into it and then send him on a "flight" across the room. He usually aimed for the pillows at the head of the bed, but, more often than not, Hobo and the helmet would part company in midair. Hobo would then have to scramble to get his feet under him. This always made Toby laugh. Usually Hobo landed on the bed, but sometimes he would "crash" and land in a pile of toys on the floor. That hurt, and Hobo would dash under the bed. Hobo learned, very soon, that he could escape from Toby under the bed. Toby had to crawl on his stomach to get at him. As soon as Toby was under the bed, Hobo would scramble up on top of it. By the time Toby had wriggled his way out from under the bed and was in a position to grab him, Hobo would dart under again. Toby would try to entice the puppy out by using a gentle tone of voice and saying nice things to him, like Marsha did, things like, "You're a cutie. Yes, I'm going to give you your bone to chew on. Yes. Good boy. Come on over here."

Hobo fell for this line a couple of times and each time he was sorry. As soon as Toby got hold of him, he would tie the poor dog up to a truck or send him on a space flight again. And, of course, he never got the bone to chew on. That didn't really matter so much, because as soon as Toby tired of playing with him, he would tune into the TV and Hobo was free to select any toy he wanted for chewing on. His two favorites were the leather baseball mitt and a small, wooden truck that would roll away when he pounced on it. Then he would stalk it stealthily and pounce. If he knocked it over, it gave up and wouldn't try to get away anymore and he could chew on a corner of it. Sometimes Hobc became so intent on his chewing that he was not aware that Toby was sneaking up on him. It was Toby who would then pounce and for Hobo it was time again to pull trucks and play Astronaut.

Another game Toby liked to play was Sea Monster. He had to get Mrs. Patterson's permission for this because it took place in the bathtub. Mrs. Patterson tried to discourage this game. It always made a mess. Toby would wait until one of Mrs. Patterson's favorite programs was on, then he would ask to play Sea Monster and threaten a tantrum if she wouldn't let him. He always got his way. Mrs. Patterson could never handle a tantrum during one of her favorite TV shows.

There was a large plastic basket in the bathroom. It contained a variety of wooden and plastic boats that Toby took into the tub with him whenever he had to have a bath. To play this game, Toby would fill the tub with water. Then he would put in all of his boats. Next he would put in Hobo.

The puppy would thrash around in the tub and sink the boats one after another. This amused Toby greatly. He would make up disaster stories that went along with the events and shout them out to himself.

"Tidal wave! Tidal wave! The monster's making a tidal wave! There's no escape! We're going to sink! Blub, blub, blub . . . all hands lost at sea." Toby would then dump water out of that particular boat, refloat it, and wait for the monster to sink it again.

Standing on his hind legs, Hobo could always keep his head above water, but he could not get out of the tub. The slippery sides were too high. He had to stay in the water until Toby tired of the game and lifted him out. The first time they played Sea Monster, Toby left the bathroom door open. Hobo dashed out dripping wet and shook himself a number of times in front of the sofa in the living room. Mrs. Patterson screamed as ice cold water sprayed all over her. Hobo rolled on the rug to get dryer and made a big wet spot. After that, one of the rules of Sea Monster was that the bathroom door had to be kept closed until after Hobo had shaken himself and rubbed himself dry on the bathroom mat. Sometimes Toby forgot about him in there and Hobo had to wait a long time. He didn't like the bathroom. The floor was cold and damp. There was nothing to do there. There was nothing to chew on. He'd whine or bark, but Toby and Mrs. Patterson were so tuned in to their TV sets that they seldom heard him. He'd almost rather take his chances in Toby's room than play Sea Monster in the tub.

Hobo liked the afternoons best when he could go to the park. Even if he had to stay leashed to the bench with Mrs. Patterson it was better than being tormented by Toby.

Things went along this way for a few months. But then it began to get cold. It rained a lot and sometimes it snowed. Mrs. Patterson didn't go to the park very often. She hated sitting on a bench in the cold, and would use any excuse to stay in the apartment.

For Hobo, this turn of events was bad news. The park was his only relief from Toby. All day in that room with him was too much to take. But there was one compensation. Hobo was not a little puppy anymore. Dogs grow a lot faster than boys. Hobo was almost his full size at six months old. When he first arrived, Toby could pick him up and carry him around. Toby could hardly lift him now, and then only if Hobo cooperated, which he didn't do very often. Hobo grew too large for space flights and as soon as he saw Toby tying string to anything, he ducked under the bed. Toby tried hard to think of some new game he could play with this oversized puppy. He was mulling over a number of possibilities when, suddenly, this weird idea came to him.

Toby had one white dress shirt that he wore only for very special occasions. His mother insisted that he wear it, with a tie, whenever they visited her uncle, who was quite old, exceedingly rich, and extremely fussy about clothes. Since Uncle Carlton never married and had no children, Marsha was hopeful that, if Toby made a good impression, Uncle Carlton might remember him in his will. Since these visits took place only a few times each year, Toby hardly ever wore the shirt and tie.

Struck with this sudden inspiration, Toby got the shirt out of the closet. With gentle words he began to pet Hobo, who was snoozing peacefully on the bed. Toby scratched

Hobo's tummy and the dog rolled over on his back. Hobo loved having his tummy scratched. Gently, Toby put one front paw through the sleeve of the shirt. Then he slowly rolled Hobo over, into the shirt, and onto his back again. All the time Toby spoke softly and scratched his tummy. In this way, he got the other front paw into the other sleeve of the shirt. Of course, the sleeves were much too long for Hobo's legs and dangled off the ends of his paws. Toby buttoned up the shirt and tied the necktie around the collar. Since he didn't know how to do it properly, he just made a granny knot. One end came out much longer than the other. Toby looked at Hobo lying on his back, with his shirt and tie on. He looked ridiculous. Toby smiled a mischievous smile. Gently he took the loose ends of the shirtsleeves and tied them together with another granny knot. Hobo was now in a kind of straitjacket, with his front paws pretty much immobilized.

Toby stopped the petting and the soft words. Suddenly he shouted, "Bounce! Here, Bounce!" Hobo flipped over and tried to stand, but his front end collapsed under him. Toby broke into gales of laughter. Hobo tried to walk, but he couldn't. His front paws didn't work. He fell on his face. This brought more laughter from Toby. Hobo struggled to get his front paws free, but all he could do was thrash around on the bed. He thrashed around so much that he rolled off the bed and crashed into a pile of trucks and cars on the floor. Toby was beside himself with laughter.

Hobo was mad now. He growled at the shirt and attacked the knotted sleeves with his teeth, but without the use of his front paws he lost his balance and fell over into the trucks and cars again. He tried to scramble under the bed, but his hind paw stepped on the long end of the necktie. He tripped and his head went down hard on the floor. Toby's laughter was uncontrollable. Hobo got madder. He rolled over on his back and started to attack the knotted sleeves with his hind paws. His claws caught in the shirt fabric and ripped it. He snatched a loose end with his teeth and pulled. He shook his head furiously. Lying on his back this way, using both his hind feet and his teeth, he shredded those shirt-sleeves to pieces. Then he got his back feet inside the shirt and pushed against the fabric. His claws caught and ripped it. Buttons came flying off. With his front paws now free, he got hold of the long end of the necktie and ripped it up with his teeth. With tooth and claw, Hobo reduced that shirt and tie to rags in about three minutes. Toby stopped laughing as he looked down at the destroyed shirt and tie. He got the remains off the dog as quickly as possible and stuffed them under his mattress. He'd figure out what to tell his mother later.

Toby had his usual lunch of a peanut butter and jelly sandwich with a Coke. It was cold and raining out so there would be no going to the park. After lunch Mrs. Patterson plugged into her favorite TV soap opera. Toby was bored. He hadn't played "sea monster" for a long time. This was the perfect moment to get Mrs. Patterson's approval.

"Okay, okay. But no mess, okay?"

"Okay," said Toby and started filling the tub. Since Hobo was now too big to carry, Toby had to get the leash and drag him into the bathroom. Once in there, Toby looped the leash over one of the washbasin faucet handles. Next he started launching his fleet. "Too bad, suckers," he said to the imaginary crews. "The monster is bigger than ever now. It's going to be a short trip to the bottom for all hands." Toby unsnapped Hobo's leash and pulled him over to the tub. "Come on, monster!" Hobo was reluctant to play the game, but Toby had a firm grip on his skin. By pulling and pushing, he managed to hoist the dog up and over the side of the tub. There was a great splash. Most of the fleet went down immediately. Hobo was big enough now to stand on the bottom with all fours and keep his head above water. He turned around to face Toby, leaving more sunk boats in his wake. The water felt cool and good, so Hobo just stood there looking at Toby and lapping up a few mouthfuls of water to quench his thirst. Toby dumped all the water out of the sunk boats and set them floating again. Hobo just stood there. "Come on, monster. Do your stuff!" Hobo did nothing. Tony splashed water in his face. Hobo closed his eyes and licked it up. "Come on! Make waves! Sink the fleet!" Toby started pushing and pulling at Hobo. Hobo sat down in the water. "I'll make you play, you dumb dog." Toby was losing his temper. He took both his hands and forced Hobo's head under water. The reaction was immediate. Hobo pulled back and jumped clear out of the tub. He sunk a lot of boats in the process and he knocked Toby over, which was a great surprise to both of them. The bathroom door was closed, but not on the latch. Hobo jumped against it and was out. He dashed into the living room and shook.

"Toby! You broke the rule! The puppy is out!" Mrs. Patterson was both shouting and trying to stay dry at the same time. Toby ran into the living room just as Hobo shook again. The boy shrank back as the cold water hit him.

"Catch him!" ordered Mrs. Patterson, shielding herself from the spray.

Toby made a dive for Hobo, but the dog was quicker. The cold dip in the tub and a couple of good shakes had restored Hobo's spirit. He felt wild and free. He put his front paws flat out in front of him, lowered his head between his paws, and barked at Toby. Despite the shakes, Hobo was still very wet and was rapidly dripping a big spot on the rug.

"You better catch him!" commanded Mrs. Patterson from behind the sofa.

Toby was a little afraid. The dog suddenly seemed almost as big as he was. "You help me," he said quietly.

"This is the last time you'll play in the water. The puppy is too big now." As soon as Mrs. Patterson approached, Hobo went like a shot past her and up on the sofa. He was too big to get under it anymore. He stood there dripping, with his paws up on the back of the sofa, barking at the two humans. "Get off! You'll wet the sofa!" shouted Mrs. Patterson. She started to come after him, but he jumped off the sofa in one bound and raced around and around in tight circles in the middle of the living room. He was having a ball. Nobody was going to catch him today. "Puppy, you're crazy," said Mrs. Patterson in bewilderment. Then, changing her mood to angry again, she shouted to Toby, "You catch him or I'm gonna tell your Mama!"

Cautiously, Toby moved closer to the circling dog. Suddenly, Hobo broke from his pattern and dashed past Mrs. Patterson. She bent over to grab him, but he was too fast. Instead, she knocked over a standing lamp that was on.

When it hit the floor, the bulb popped with a loud noise and a blue flash that scared them all. Mrs. Patterson reached for the wall to steady herself, but she was next to a window and the "wall" was a curtain which came down when she grabbed it, along with the curtain rod. Mrs. Patterson was breathless. In this moment of startled calm, Toby made another dive for the dog. He missed, but hit the corner of a small end table, knocking it over. Unfortunately, there was a china vase full of flowers on top of the table. Broken china, flowers, and a lot more water were now on the rug. Unfortunately, Toby also hit the table with his nose which started to bleed. Toby had never had a nosebleed before. The sight of his shirt becoming stained with his own blood caused him to cry out in hysterics. Mrs. Patterson told him to be careful not to get blood on the sofa or on the rug. She went into the kitchen and came back with a large bundle of paper towels. She placed paper towels, double thick, on the back of the sofa and made Toby sit with his head resting in the middle of the towels. She gave him a fistful more to hold over his nose. Then she turned her attention back to the TV soap opera, which was just coming to its final crisis. The room was a shambles. Toby had a bloody nose. The dog was still dripping wet. But Mrs. Patterson was determined to see the end of her soap.

Hobo, sensing that the game was over and that he had won, decided it was time to make up and be friends. Gently he jumped up on the sofa to snuggle in between Toby and Mrs. Patterson. Since he was still quite damp, his attentions were greeted by a loud squawk and a shove by Mrs. Patterson and a sharp kick from Toby. The kick sent Hobo reeling back on the floor and also started up Toby's nosebleed again, which brought on more hysterical cries, which caused Mrs. Patterson to miss the last spoken lines of the soap.

Mrs. Patterson was furious. Now she would have to wait until the next day to find out whether the talented young artist would recover from the emergency brain operation that he had just undergone because of a motorcycle accident caused by his best friend, who had had too much to drink at a party for the artist's girl friend, whose father didn't approve of the young artist seeing his daughter and who also just happened to be the brain surgeon.

When Marsha and Allan got home that evening, there was a big scene. Mrs. Patterson threatened to quit. Toby laid all the blame for the smashed vase, the broken lamp, the torn curtains, his bloody nose, and even his ruined shirt and tie completely on Hobo. "The puppy went crazy," said Mrs. Patterson. The next day, Hobo found himself back in a cage at the animal shelter.

THIRD NAME, "SAM"

THE FIRST DAY BACK IN THE CAGE AT THE shelter, Hobo felt, was almost a relief. There was no Toby to tie strings to him, or to push his head under water, or to wrap him up in clothes. It was very peaceful in the cage. Not a quiet kind of peaceful; there were too many dogs in the room for that, but just to be left alone was peaceful. Nobody who came to the shelter looking for a pet paid any attention to Hobo.

The second day, Hobo grew restless. Being in the cage was a bore. The cage seemed to be much smaller than he remembered it. He couldn't stand on his hind legs with his front paws against the door and bark and wag his tail to get attention. He tried it once and bumped his head hard on the roof of his cage. All he could do was just stand quietly on all fours, or sit, or lie down. He wanted to move about and be lively, but he couldn't. He was too big to do that in this cage anymore. Nobody asked to see him the second day either.

The third day, Hobo felt even worse. He just lay in his cage and tried to snooze to pass the time faster. In the afternoon an older man and his wife came to the shelter. They told the attendant that their dog, Sam, had died recently of old age and had left a big emptiness in their life. They wanted another dog as much like Sam as possible. Since Sam had been a shaggy dog, the attendant took them over to Hobo's cage. He was quietly snoozing when the man asked the attendant to take the dog out so they could see him better. Once out of the cage, Hobo stretched, yawned, and felt better. The man and the woman, whose names were Harold and Alice, seemed friendly and pleasant. Hobo wagged his tail and licked their hands as they petted him.

"He's much like Sam, isn't he?" Harold was saying.

"He's not as big, but in our tiny apartment, that's all to the good." Alice had a smile in her voice. "And he seems to have such a nice personality."

"Let's take him."

"Yes. You'd like to come live with us, wouldn't you, Sam?"

"You called him Sam," said Harold, quite surprised.

"I did, didn't I? Well, that settles it. Sam he is. Oh, Harold, I feel so good about him."

Harold smiled and squeezed her hand.

"I'm glad you're taking him," said the attendant. "He seems like a good dog and if someone hadn't taken him today, he would have been destroyed. We can't keep them more than three days, you know. There are so many, we are overwhelmed."

"Why, that's terrible!" Alice was shocked.

"I'm glad we're taking him too," said Harold as he filled out the forms.

Harold and Alice lived in a small apartment near a park. Hobo was now completely house-trained and never spotted a rug or made any mistakes, ever. He preferred the park. This park was larger than the one that Hobo had visited with Toby and Mrs. Patterson. This was the main park of the city. Hobo and Alice took long walks in the park every day, rain or shine, and also in the snow. Hobo enjoyed these walks, even though she never let him off the leash. However, Alice was much more understanding about smells than either Mrs. Patterson or Larry. Sam must have trained her well. If Hobo hesitated by a particularly interesting aroma, she would stop and let him savor it, saying, "If it's really that good, Lovey, okay, but don't take all day." She called him Lovey when she didn't call him Sam. She was so gentle and understanding that he didn't mind walking with the leash on at all. Well, not quite "at all." There were a number of times when Hobo wished he was free of that leash. These were the times when he would encounter a cat or a squirrel. Some basic dog instinct took over then and he would charge out to the end of the leash after either one of those two animals. They always ran away scared, but he hated being jerked up short when he had them on the run.

Alice was an artist. She drew pictures for greeting cards. They usually featured a shaggy dog doing something silly.

She was very good at drawing shaggy dogs. She worked in a corner of the living room. There was a drawing table with a top that tilted to just the right angle so that Alice didn't have to hunch over her work. Near the drawing table was a large red leather chair. This was Hobo's favorite place. He was a perfect fit when he curled up in it. It made just the right Hobo-sized nest. Sometimes, if he wanted to stretch out, he would drape himself over the edge of the chair. Often, he would sleep on his back, diagonally across the chair, with his head hanging over the edge, upside down. He could also sit in the chair with the back supporting him, just like a person. Although he didn't know why, he always felt quite important when he sat in the chair this way.

Alice would often look at Hobo in his chair, smile, and quickly move her pencil over the paper on her drawing board, sketching the position that he was in. When she was finished, she would always show him what she had drawn. "Here, Lovey, how do you like your portrait?" He would always sniff at it politely and give a couple of tail wags to show his appreciation, but actually it smelled and looked like a piece of paper with some lead pencil marks on it, so he never got very excited about the drawings she made of him. Alice would put the paper down on the board again, look at him in a loving way, ruffle up the hair on his head, and say, "I'd give a lot to know what goes on in that head of yours, you know that?" Then she'd go back to her drawing board.

Harold worked in the office of a big department store. He was an accountant. He kept track of all the money that the store took in and all that it paid out. Harold was very good at math. He liked to say that both he and Alice were sharp pencil people. Then he'd kid her and say that his pencil had been replaced by an electronic calculator and he was just waiting for the day when Alice's drawings would be done by a computer. Then Alice would say, "Over my dead body," and go fix their supper.

Hobo lived with Harold and Alice all that winter. Nothing very exciting happened. Life was peaceful and pleasant. Life was the exact opposite of what it had been with Toby. As winter gave way to spring, however, Hobo sensed a new mood in the air. He wanted to be out more. He wanted to be off the leash. He was bored with the pleasant routine. He was restless.

It was a Sunday toward the end of May. It was the first hot day of the year. Harold and Alice had eaten a late breakfast and then gone into the park together with Hobo. He had never seen so many people in the park before. It was like the entire city had decided to go to the park on this lovely, clear, hot day. There were people pushing baby carriages and people pedaling bikes. There were people on roller skates and people on the grass. There were people walking and sitting and lying down. There were old people and young people and children and babies. There were people flying kites and throwing frisbees and playing ball. Everywhere were people enjoying this beautiful day. And there were also dogs. Even in the shelter, Hobo had never seen so many dogs. The park was full of people and their dogs. There were also squirrels and pigeons. There was so much to see and hear and smell that Hobo couldn't keep it all sorted out. The whole scene became one big, exciting, blur of activity. Every living thing, the people, the dogs, the squirrels, and even the pigeons, seemed especially happy to be alive on this particular day.

Alice and Harold found two unoccupied places on a bench. They sat down, leaned their heads back, and soaked up the sun. Hobo lay at their feet for a while, but there was so much going on all around him that he found it hard to lie still. A ball would roll his way and he had to go try to pick it up. A squirrel or a pigeon would come close and he had to chase them, at least as far as his leash would go. Any number of dogs would pass by and he just had to get acquainted. He was up and down tugging on his leash so often that finally Harold, who was holding the other end, bent down and released him, saying, "I know you want to run. And I would too, if I were a young fellow like you. But Alice and I, we just want to stay quietly here and soak up the sun."

"Be a good boy, Lovey. Don't go far," added Alice.

Hobo dashed away. He ran as fast as he could in a big circle around the bench. It felt good all over just to run at top speed around and around. A ball came bounding past and he changed directions to run after it. He grabbed it in his mouth, turned, and stopped. Two boys came running over. "Hey! Drop it!" one of them shouted. Hobo just looked at him with the ball in his mouth. It didn't taste very good; nevertheless, he wasn't about to give it up immediately. He wanted to play. As soon as the boys got close, Hobo ran off a little way. They tried to catch him, but he would always stay just out of reach. From his months of living with Toby, he knew all about how *not* to get caught.

He played this game with the two boys until one of them got angry.

"Drop it! Dumb dog! Let's throw some stones at him. Then maybe he'll drop it."

"Wait a minute," said the other boy. "He's just playing. Let's use a little psychology." He bent down and started coaxing Hobo over with a gentle manner. "Hey, fella. You're a good boy, aren't you? Come over here. I'd like to pet you. Yes . . . good boy." Hobo came over and dropped the ball. The boy gave him a few pats on the head and said, "Good boy" again.

"Okay, come on, toss it here. Let's play." The two boys ran off, throwing the ball to each other.

Hobo stretched. That had been fun. A golden retriever trotted over. It was a girl golden retriever. They sniffed noses and got acquainted. Hobo felt like showing off. He raced around the golden retriever in ever-widening circles. When a bench got in his way, he jumped right over it. He even surprised himself at how well he could jump. The retriever was obviously impressed and they trotted off together with the retriever leading the way. They went further and further from the bench where Harold and Alice were sitting. Finally, they came to a young couple with two little children. The father said sternly, "Natasha! Where have you been? We've been looking all over for you. We've got to go. Hey! Who's your furry friend?" He clipped a leash on Natasha and they all started out of the park along the roadway.

Hobo watched them go. Then he decided that he'd better head back to find Harold and Alice. But he saw this squirrel chattering at him and twitching its tail in a taunting manner. Hobo froze. Every nerve and muscle in his body became tense. His nose, his eyes, and his ears were all concentrated on that squirrel. Something deep inside Hobo told him that this was the most fun of all the games. This was the hunt!

Ever so slowly he lowered his body and lifted his paws. Ever so slowly, he moved forward. He had to move as if he weren't moving at all and at the same time keep every muscle tensed and ready to pounce with all possible speed and power. It was an exciting thing to be doing. Closer and closer he crept. The squirrel just sat there on its hind legs, watching Hobo with its bright, black eyes, twitching its tail, and making silly chatter. Hobo was so close now that he was ready to pounce. In an instant, the squirrel had turned and dashed up a tree. Hobo dashed after it, but the squirrel was too quick. There it was now on the lowest limb of the tree, directly over Hobo, chattering at him and twitching its tail. Hobo danced on his hind legs right under the squirrel and barked. The two of them chattered and barked at each other for a whole minute or two. Then Hobo dropped his front paws to the ground and jumped straight up as high as he could. He came very close to catching that squirrel. If its tail had been hanging down, he might just have gotten it. In any case, he gave it such a scare that it scampered up to the top of the tree and kept quiet.

Hobo was feeling great. So he didn't catch that smarty squirrel. Maybe he taught it a lesson and, anyhow, what would he have done with it if he had caught it? It was a glorious day. He'd had some exciting fun, played tag with two boys, made friends with a girl golden retriever, and almost caught a squirrel. Not bad for the first day off the leash in the park! And he had the whole summer before him. Life never felt better than at this very moment.

He was trotting along the side of the roadway, heading back toward the bench where he'd left Alice and Harold, when he passed an old beat-up van that was parked by the side of the road. Suddenly, Hobo felt rough hands in heavy leather gloves grab him and toss him into the back of the van. The door slammed shut. Another man jabbed something sharp into Hobo's backside. Everything began to get hazy and slipped into darkness. The last thing Hobo remembered was the van driving off and Alice's voice calling, "Sam! Here, Sam! Where are you, Lovey!"

When Hobo came to, he was back in a cage again, only this wasn't the animal shelter. The cage was rusty. The place was filthy and smelled of chemicals and sick animals. The room was full of cages stacked on top of each other, and the cages were full of cats and dogs. Some looked like purebreds, but most were mixed breeds like Hobo. Almost all of them had patches of their hair shaved off. The exposed skin was blistery and looked like it must be very sore. Many animals whimpered and cried. The sound was awful. Some seemed to be dead or almost dead. Hobo stood up. His rear leg, up high where the needle went in, hurt. He could hardly stand on all fours, his cage was so small. Below him was a row of bigger cages where the larger dogs were kept. Above him was a row of even smaller cages where the little dogs and cats were kept. Up near the ceiling was a row of windows covered with rusty screening. A large fan hung down from the middle of the ceiling. It turned slowly, but it wasn't very successful at blowing out the smell or cooling the room.

Hobo turned around in his cage and stretched the leg that hurt. Even though it hurt more to do so, Hobo sensed that this was the right thing to do, and the more he used it, the less it hurt. He took a little satisfaction in that. Then he realized that he was very hungry. He had no idea how long he had been in this place. There was daylight coming through the windows, but whether it was the same day, or the next, or many days since he had wandered away from Harold and Alice in the park, Hobo couldn't tell. His stomach was empty, that much was certain, but at the same time the stench in the room and the sight of all those sick cats and dogs made the thought of food repulsive. He couldn't eat anything even if it were placed right in front of him. It was a terrible feeling.

The swinging door to the room opened. A man and woman, dressed in dirty, white smocks, entered. The man was telling the woman to take out number 73. "He's a long hair. Don't shave him. The lab wants to test this new hair dye for possible cancer effects. We want to see the reaction on both his skin and his hair. Apply it 100 times normal strength on the usual nine-square-inch area. Work it in well through the hair, because the skin reaction is important too."

The man left. The woman walked over to Hobo's cage, slipped a noose-type leash over his head, and lifted him out. She was wearing rubber gloves. The stains on her smock smelled awful. She put Hobo down on the floor. He realized that his old collar, with his name and dog tags, was gone. The woman led him out through the swinging door into another, smaller, room. There was a metal table here, and glass containers full of gooey liquids. There were brushes and a box of hypodermic needles on a shelf. A chemical smell, even worse than in the cage room, hung over everything. As they walked, the woman kept a slight upward pull on the leash, so that Hobo was near choking all the time. She led him to the table and lifted him up onto it.

"You're a pussycat, aren't you?" Her words were sweet, but her manner was rough. Her way with him reminded him of Toby. He took an instant dislike to her. "You're not going to give me a hard time, are you? I'm not going to have to waste an injection on you, like I do with those big shaved dogs, now am I? That's it, just be easy now."

Hobo looked at her with a friendly face, but all his nerves and muscles were as tense as if he were stalking that squirrel. He was ready for anything.

With one hand, she kept a firm upward pressure on the leash; with the other she dipped a wide brush into some thick, brown goo and spread it over a part of Hobo's back. Then she got a second brush full and worked the brown goo in until it slathered on Hobo's skin. It stung like crazy.

Hobo had never snapped at anybody before in his life, not even Toby, but now he sank his teeth into the hand that held the brush and shook furiously. The woman screamed in surprise and pain. Hobo had seemed to be such a gentle dog. The brush full of brown goo flipped out of her hand and slopped against the sleeve of her smock. It soaked in and touched her skin. She screamed even louder and let go of the leash. Hobo jumped from the table and dashed through the swinging doors back into the cage room. The goo on his back felt like fire. Even though it hurt, he jumped up onto the top of the first row of big cages. He jumped again up onto the top row of the middle-sized cages. And he jumped up onto the very top row of little cages. The windows, covered with rusty screens, were still high above him. He could hear angry voices coming through the swinging door.

"Stupid mutt!"

"Where is he?"

"Up on top. The dumb dog is up on top!"

"Don't let him get away!"

"Come on, after him!"

Two men started to climb up the cages. For just a moment, Hobo watched them scramble up, cursing and shouting. Then, in one leap, he made it out through the rusty screens to the roof outside. He ran as fast as he could. He was on top of a row of old, brick buildings. It was a hot, humid day. The tar on the roof was soft and burned the pads on his paws. He couldn't stop if he wanted to. He just kept running. He heard the men in the cage room shouting about getting a ladder, but Hobo never looked back. He reached the edge of the roof. There was an air shaft about four feet wide between the buildings. Without thinking, he jumped it. He just kept going over the roofs of the row of buildings, leaping the air shafts and low walls between buildings. Finally, he came to the end of the block of old buildings. There was a fire escape ladder here. Hobo had learned to climb up and down stairs when he was just a puppy, but this was different. The steps were much narrower and steeper. It was open all around. The street was so far below. Well, there was no turning back. He hadn't liked playing Bombs Away with Toby, but maybe it was good training. He wasn't as afraid of heights as he once was.

He scrambled down the first ladder. He didn't look to one side or the other. He didn't look beyond the next step down where he had to put his paws. He didn't think about anything except getting down to the street and away from this terrible place. He scrambled down six stories to the ground level. The last few feet he jumped. He hit the sidewalk and kept going. He reached the end of the block and kept going. He heard the shouts of people and the squeal of brakes as he dashed across the street, but he kept going. He ran for a number of blocks, never stopping for anything. He was almost hit a couple of times by cars and trucks, but he kept going, full tilt. He came to a place near an auto shop where somebody had drained their car radiator. There was a puddle of smelly, oily water by the curb. Hobo's strength had given out. He fell into the puddle and rolled in the oily water. The wetness was good, but the patch of goo still stung like crazy. Hobo was so exhausted and hungry and hurting that he passed out in that stinking, oily puddle. Somebody passing by thought that he was dead and made a telephone call.

The next thing Hobo knew was that he was being picked up by a pair of leather gloves and put in the back of a van again. There were a few other scruffy-looking dogs already there. Hobo was sure that he was being taken back to the testing laboratory with the chemical smells and the brush that stung. But his spirit was all gone. He was so weak that he couldn't do a thing to save himself. The van stopped and two men with heavy leather gloves lifted him out of the van and carried him into a room with a metal table in the middle of it. Hobo waited for the needle to jab into him or to feel that terrible brush full of brown goo. Instead, a man in a clean, white jacket came over and looked at him.

"The caller said that he was dead?"

"That's right, doctor," one of the men from the van answered. "And I'll tell you, he looked more dead than alive when we found him."

Hobo did look like some kind of drowned animal, one perhaps that had been drowned in an oil spill somewhere. His hair was matted together with the antifreeze from the drained radiator. He was a soaking wet mess. As the doctor examined him, he came upon the area where the brown goo had been brushed into his skin. The doctor became quite excited and called his assistant over.

"Bring me some swabs. I think we finally have one that's escaped from that testing lab."

The assistant brought over a number of wooden sticks with tufts of cotton on one end. Very gently, the doctor swabbed off the brown goo from Hobo's skin and hair. He was careful not to get his fingers in the goo. He was also careful to place the swabs on a clean glass plate. Even though he was very gentle, when the swabs touched Hobo's skin it hurt and Hobo winced. When the doctor had finished, the two men from the van put Hobo in a concrete shower area and thoroughly washed him and rinsed him down. Hobo was so weak that one of the men had to hold him up. Then they toweled him dry and brought him food and water. The pads on his paws still hurt from the hot tar on the roof, so Hobo lay down while he lapped up some of the food and water. A little later, the doctor came back and examined the place where the brown goo had been. He put some medical cream on it and that made it feel better.

"He's definitely from the lab. The material on the test patch appears to be some kind of hair dye for humans, but at many times normal strength. I'd love to locate that lab. Tell me again where you found him."

The van driver, who was still with Hobo, gave the doctor the location of the oily puddle.

"I wonder how far he traveled before he collapsed."

"It could have been a long way," the driver replied. "Here's the leash that was on him. No identification, of course. But stuck in his hair around the leash was this small piece of rusty screening. Looks like he went through a window or a door. Also, it hurts him to stand. I checked and found tar on the pads of his feet. I'll bet the lab is on the roof of some building in that area."

"It all helps," said the doctor as he left.

Hobo was gently carried to another room full of cages, but this room was bright and clean. He was put in a spotless cage made of stainless steel. Hobo was in the hospital section of the city's main animal shelter. He promptly went to sleep and slept for the better part of two days.

There were a number of different animal shelters in the city. Each one was run by a different organization. Alice called them all asking if anyone had brought in a dog that looked like Sam. But she called the Sunday that Sam disappeared and then the following Monday and Tuesday. These were the days that Hobo was probably at the laboratory.

Alice didn't think to call the hospital. As the days went by, she and Harold became resigned to the fact that they would never see their dog again.

The doctor visited Hobo in the hospital every day and examined the area where the brown goo had been applied. From the rapid way that he recovered, the doctor figured that the test material could not have been on Hobo's skin for very long before he was picked up, probably not more than ten or fifteen minutes. That narrowed down the area where the lab could be located.

One day, after Hobo had been in the hospital for about a week, the doctor took him out of the cage and examined the spot as usual, but Hobo sensed that there was something special about this day. The doctor seemed excited.

"Well, my friend," he said, talking to Hobo, "you're going to be just fine. You may lose a few hairs and that patch of skin will be sensitive for a while, but you'll be all right very soon. I wish I could say the same for those other animals from the testing lab. Thanks to you, we located the place. The animals are on their way here now and the police have started an investigation. If it isn't a crime to steal animals for that kind of wretched testing, it certainly ought to be. So you, my friend, are dismissed from the hospital. We're going to put you up for adoption. I wish I could take you home myself, but my wife would throw *me* out! We've got four dogs and three cats as it is. I wish you lots of luck. You deserve it."

An attendant took Hobo down some long corridors. It was the first time he'd really done any walking since he escaped from the lab. The pads of his paws didn't hurt anymore. Everything seemed to be working just fine. The attendant took him to the adoption wing of the shelter and put him in another cage in a room mostly full of puppies again. This wasn't the same place that he had been before. It was a different shelter in a different part of the city.

FOURTH NAME, "SHAG"

MORE THAN A YEAR HAD PASSED SINCE HOBO had first scrambled over the edge of the puppy box and pounced on a green pea in Mrs. Billingswort's kitchen. Her favorite of the litter was now an adult dog, sitting in a cage at an animal shelter, competing with a room full of cute puppies, waiting for someone to adopt him. The puppies were so lively and cuddly, they were the obvious choice of anyone coming to the shelter. Every day people came and took a number of the puppies home with them. Nobody picked Hobo. At the end of the third day the doctor visited him again. He brought a woman named Janet with him. She was the director of the adoption center. She was speaking quite firmly.

"Doctor, I understand you feel especially fond of this particular animal. But it has been our stated policy for some time now to destroy animals that are not adopted by the end of the seventy-two-hour stay at the shelter. And, I'm afraid, this animal's time is up."

"Janet, I understand the problem of too many unwanted pets and no place to put them, and I admit I am especially fond of this dog, but that's not the point. I feel he deserves better than our normal, 'business as usual' treatment. If it hadn't been for him, I doubt if we ever would have located that inhumane testing lab. He's a kind of a hero in my book."

"Hero or not, he's a middle-aged mutt. People want puppies to take home with them. He could be stuck in that cage for years. And that would not be fair to him either."

"I'm not asking for that. All I would like you to do is bend the rules a little, keep him through the weekend. Give him a little more time. He's earned that, at least."

"All right, I'll hold him until Monday morning, but I honestly don't think it's going to make a bit of difference."

"Thank you, Janet. I appreciate it." The doctor opened the cage and gave Hobo a loving pat, saying, "Good luck, fella." Then he closed the cage door and left. It was a Thursday morning.

The rest of Thursday and all of Friday came and went. Nobody was the least bit interested in adopting Hobo. Saturday morning a young couple came to the shelter. The man liked Hobo, but the woman wanted a black and white spotted puppy. They had an argument. The woman won. The puppy went home with them and Hobo stayed in his cage. Sunday passed without a single person even asking about Hobo.

Monday morning the shelter opened at 9:00 A.M. A man and his wife and her ten-year-old daughter, Jill, were waiting at the door when it opened. They were looking for an older dog, the man said, one they wouldn't have to train. The attendant immediately took them to see Hobo. When they got inside, his cage was empty! The attendant made a quick phone call to her boss, Janet. There was a flurry of activity in the shelter as Hobo was located and brought back to the lobby. A few more minutes and he would have been destroyed, along with a number of other unwanted cats and dogs. He, of course, had no idea of what was going on. He was just happy to be out of his cage and to be walked up and down the shelter's corridors. He liked the exercise.

When Jill first saw him, she ran over and threw her arms around his neck. She hugged and petted him. "He's so shaggy! I love him. Please, can we take him?"

"I don't see why not, he seems to like you too, Jill." Her mother patted Hobo on the head.

"Good. I'm glad that's settled. We have a long drive ahead of us. Do you have a leash for the dog?" the man asked the attendant.

"Yes, we have them for sale," she answered. "And I'm afraid I'll have to ask you to fill out our standard adoption form. It will take only a few minutes."

"How much is the leash?" asked the man as he started to fill out the form.

"We sell them for the same price that they cost us, from $1.50 to $3.00."

"I'll take one of the $1.50 variety."

"That may be a little small for him," said the attendant, glancing over at Hobo. "He's not a tiny dog, you know, like a Pekingese or a toy poodle."

"I know," the man replied sharply, "but we'll be in the country, a real backwoods situation. We won't need the leash much."

"Oh, how nice," said the attendant, handing the man his change from the $2.00. "I hope you all have a marvelous time together."

"Thank you," said Jill's mother. "I'm so glad we came here this morning."

"Come on, Shaggy." Jill had clipped the thin, plastic leash onto Hobo's collar and was leading him toward the door.

"That's a good name for him, Jill," her mother said. "He certainly is shaggy."

Their car was parked right in front of the animal shelter. The back seat was already crowded with plastic bags and a couple of cardboard boxes containing clothes, some food, and two of Jill's favorite dolls. Jill pushed Hobo over these things into the back seat and then scrambled in beside him. She hugged and petted him and he nuzzled into her neck and licked her face.

The man, who was Jill's stepfather, started the car. Hobo tensed up. He'd never been in a passenger car before. He remembered those two vans and the memory was painful. He pulled away from Jill and nervously watched as the whole world started to move past him outside the car window.

"It's all right, Shaggy. We're going to the country." Jill petted him calmly. "Hey, Mom, I'll bet he's never been in a car before!"

Jill's mother turned around and smiled as Hobo seemed to accept being in the car and snuggled next to Jill again.

Then her smile faded as she said, "Now, you must remember, Jill, that we can't bring Shaggy back to the city with us. He's your special vacation friend because there aren't any children near us up in the mountains." She paused a moment. "And, Jill, I want you to know that the attendant at the shelter told me that if we hadn't taken Shaggy this morning, right when we did, he would have been put to sleep. They don't keep older dogs very long there. So you see, we are really doing him a big favor by taking him. And, of course, we'll find a good home for him when we leave."

Jill didn't say anything at first. She just hugged the dog harder. Then she looked at him and said, "Shaggy, here, Shaggy." Hobo had his head out the window, enjoying the wind blowing in his face. "Shag . . . here, Shag!" Jill said it louder and Hobo pulled his head inside the car. Jill petted him. "Good boy, Shag. Mom, I'm going to call him Shag. I like it better. It's easier to call."

They drove for a long time until they came to their vacation cottage in the mountains of New England. Jill and Hobo spent the month of June together. Her parents did not find a good home for Hobo when they left. They never got around to finding him any home at all. They only thought to leave him with an extra large dish of dog food as they locked up the cottage and headed back to the city.

PART THREE

HOME AT LAST!

HOBO HAD BEEN LYING IN THE MUD A LONG time as all these memories came rushing back through his half-awake mind. The bite of the steel trap was not like any other bite he had ever known. It never let go. The pain in his paw was all he could think about now. He no longer cared about anything else. He thought that he heard a voice saying something to him. But he couldn't be sure. He opened his eyes. There was a boy standing near him. He had a red scarf tied around his head. He spoke in a gentle, friendly manner.

"Hey, fella, what's the matter?" The boy stooped down beside the exhausted dog and saw the trap. "Easy, boy. I won't hurt you." The boy took the scarf from his head and slipped it around Hobo's neck to control him better. He tried to get the trap off his paw, but the steel spring that held the jaws closed was too strong. The trap was on a chain and the chain was tied to a tree. He released the chain and carried Hobo home on his shoulders. There was something in the way the boy handled him that made Hobo feel safe for the first time since he had been abandoned at the cottage.

The boy's name was Adam Norman. When the rest of the family, Peter, Adam's father, Carol, his mother, and Becky, his younger sister, saw him coming home with a dog on his shoulders and a trap hanging from the dog's paw, they all rushed to the nearest veterinarian. The doctor removed the trap and medicated and bandaged the wound. It was the doctor who called him a "summerdog," one who had been left behind by vacationing summer people. It was also the doctor who first called him a "little hobo." Becky decided that Hobo was a good name for a stray dog. The whole family agreed. And that's how Hobo got his fifth and final name.

The Normans advertised in the local paper to try and find Hobo's old family, but without success. Under Becky's and Adam's loving care, Hobo rapidly became his old self again. There was something about the way the Normans treated him, and treated each other too, that made Hobo feel good to be with them.

After two weeks, when no one had answered the ad in the newspaper, the Normans decided to keep Hobo themselves. Adam and Becky took off Hobo's bandage. His paw was just about healed. They all decided to have a special picnic to celebrate Hobo's becoming a member of the family. They roasted frankfurters on sticks over a fire and ate the first radishes to come from Carol's garden. Adam and

Becky decided that they didn't really like radishes at all. But they were all very surprised to discover that Hobo loved them. He would chew them up with great gusto and then make a face when the hot, white radish inside got on his tongue. But he liked them, for he would always bark for another. They all laughed and were happy. Adam and Becky hugged and petted Hobo so much that he knew that this was a special day. He was their dog now. No matter how many people had crossed his path, no matter how many places he'd been, he knew now, deep down inside, that finally he was home.

A NOTE FROM THE AUTHOR ABOUT THE REAL "HOBO"

The character of Hobo is based on Zoe, our family pet and the dog that appears in the book photographs and in the motion picture *Summerdog*. My wife, Sherry, and I found Zoe at the ASPCA shelter in New York City. At the shelter we were told that Zoe had been returned twice by other families and that if we brought her back she would be destroyed. We asked why such an attractive dog had been returned and they told us that Zoe was a very excitable animal who knocked down small children and jumped up on people and furniture. Since, at that moment, the dog was draped across my shoulders licking my face, I could see what they meant. Zoe seemed more like a monkey. But how could I say no to such an obvious appeal for affection? Dogs had always been a part of our household. We felt our children were old enough and experienced enough to handle Zoe. That was the name she had. We agreed to adopt her.

The first months weren't easy. Zoe not only jumped up on people and furniture, she wasn't house-trained or even paper-trained! By the time we took her in she was a very mixed-up, almost full grown dog. She had been rejected by so many people that she didn't trust anything with two legs at all. She hated to be left alone, probably thinking we would never come back. She showed her displeasure by going on our bed or on the sofa! There were times when we almost brought her back to the shelter, but the thought that this attractive, intelligent animal would be destroyed if we failed kept us at it. My wife and our two children shared the responsibility and worked with Zoe daily. In the training process, we learned that Zoe would do almost anything for a piece of cheese. And we found that she had a lot of natural abilities like climbing trees and dancing on her hind legs, which we used in the film SUMMERDOG.

Like the Normans, we are glad that our Zoe/Hobo has found a home at last.

GEORGE A. ZABRISKIE